ANNIE'S ATTIC MYSTERIES®

The Valise in the Attic

Jan Fields

Annie's®
AnniesFiction.com

Library of Congress-in-Publication Data
The Valise in the Attic / by Jan Fields
p. cm.
I. Title
2011937346

AnniesFiction.com
800-282-6643
Annie's Attic Mysteries®
Series Editors: Ken and Janice Tate
Series Creator: Stenhouse & Associates, Ridgefield, Connecticut

10 11 12 13 14 | Printed in China | 9 8 7 6 5

Annie Dawson drove slowly down Main Street. She still tended to creep along on snowy days. Though the plows had cleared the Stony Point roads well, snow still felt a little alien and dangerous after twenty-eight years in Texas. In many ways, Annie was feeling more and more at home in Maine, but snow was still her weakness.

Annie risked a glance at her watch as she turned onto Main Street. She was at least fifteen minutes early for the Hook and Needle Club meeting. Her friends had teased her ever since the first snow about being late for meetings because of her snow phobia. But they wouldn't be able to tease her today!

It was a good thing she'd planned to leave forty-five minutes early for the short drive to A Stitch in Time. LeeAnn had called just as she'd scooped Boots from a languid sprawl across Annie's project bag. Her daughter had her hands full with Christmas preparations, but the twins had insisted on calling Annie right away.

"We're on Christmas break," John had announced.

"Winter break," Joanna corrected from her extension. "Our teacher says we should be inclusive."

"Do you know what 'inclusive' means?" Annie asked.

"It means you call it winter break," Joanna said in her most long-suffering tone. "But we're making Christmas cookies."

"Mommy said we can make gingerbread monsters," John chimed in.

"Monsters?" Annie asked. "Why not nice happy gingerbread men?"

"Monsters are cooler," John explained. "I'm making sea monsters."

Annie smiled. Her grandson loved everything about the sea ever since their first visit to Stony Point. He could already name more kinds of sharks than Annie even knew existed.

"Gramma, we're working on a project," Joanna said, her voice serious. She was often the more solemn of the twins as she seemed to think deeply about things. "You have to do it too."

"What project is that?" Annie asked.

"We're going to be green for the whole winter break."

"Green?" Annie said, bewildered. "Like with face paint?"

"No, with recycling and not wasting water," Joanna said. "We're putting our supper scraps in a compost bin too."

"With worms!" John added.

"And we changed all our lightbulbs for the twisty ones."

Again John cut in. "Daddy says you still have to turn them off when you're not in a room, just like regular lights."

Joanna firmly tried to take the conversation back in hand. "Do you have cloth shopping bags, Gramma?"

"Around here somewhere," Annie said, knowing she also had a kitchen drawer stuffed with plastic bags from the grocery in town. "And I always put out my recycling bin."

"You have to use the cloth bags," Joanna insisted. "Please, Gramma, it's important to our planet."

"OK, I'll be extra careful," Annie assured her.

Then John chimed in that he had tried to do his part by taking fewer baths. "Mom wouldn't let me though," he grumbled.

Annie laughed at his disappointed tone. Chatting with her grandchildren was always the highlight of her day. She was so glad that LeeAnn had been able to bring the kids to see her now that she was living at Grey Gables, and that she'd been able to go back to see them in Texas. She wanted John and Joanna to have the kind of happy memories of Stony Point that she had from her own childhood and to always share their lives with her.

The whole phone conversation had gone so nicely, Annie thought to herself as she pulled into a space in front of A Stitch in Time. LeeAnn had finally accepted that Annie wasn't moving back to Texas, and now LeeAnn just liked being filled in on what Annie and her friends were doing.

"Any new mysteries, Mom?" LeeAnn had asked Annie when she had finally got the phone back from the twins.

"Only the mystery of how I'm going to get my last few Christmas gifts collected and mailed in time," Annie replied. "How would you feel about celebrating a gift-giving New Year?"

LeeAnn laughed into the phone. "You can't fool me, Mom. You always fret and insist you're not going to get done in time for the holidays. And then you always do."

Annie had to admit that was true. "It's a habit I got from your great-grandmother," Annie said. "But at least she had an excuse. Gram always had such huge Christmas parties."

"I remember a few of them," LeeAnn said.

The reminiscing left Annie with a warm glow that even

the icy chill of a Maine winter couldn't blow away. Then a sudden movement next to her window caused Annie to jump. Alice MacFarlane was standing beside the car, waving. Annie opened the door and her best friend grinned at her. "Are you coming inside?"

Annie laughed. "Yes, sorry. I was woolgathering."

"It's a good day for it," Alice said with a gasp as an icy wind rushed by them both. "The more wool the better. I'm already having spring fantasies."

"I don't know," Annie said as they walked through the half-frozen slush to the sidewalk. "As long as I'm not out in it, I love looking at it. Snow is so beautiful and makes the world look more peaceful. Besides, I think my blood is finally thickening. The first winter here almost froze me to death."

Warmth rushed out to greet them as they pulled open the door to A Stitch in Time. Annie stomped her boots on the threshold, and then walked in. The smiling faces of her friends Mary Beth Brock and Kate Stevens warmed her almost as much as the cozy temperature Mary Beth kept the little shop at. Even in the off-season, A Stitch in Time was so popular that she had to keep the heat turned up to offset the arctic blasts coming in whenever the door opened.

"You didn't spill the secret?" Mary Beth asked. "You know Peggy will be disappointed if you did."

"Mum's the word." Alice mimed turning a lock over her lips.

"What secret?" Annie asked.

"Mmmm … mmmm … mmmm," Alice said, her lips firmly shut.

"You're just too funny," Annie scolded, but she laughed.

"So will I find out when Peggy gets here?"

"You will," Mary Beth said. "Probably that very second."

"Then I can wait," Annie said.

"You're very brave," her friend said, her eyes sparkling. Each time Mary Beth moved, Annie heard the tinkling of tiny bells. Mary Beth wore a red crocheted vest that Annie had thought was decorated with red studs; now she realized they were actually tiny jingle bells.

"Your vest is darling," Annie said. "Very festive."

"Thank you. Kate made it," Mary Beth said. "I told her people would love it. You wouldn't believe the compliments I've gotten."

"I thought people might think it was tacky with all those bells," Kate said.

"No, it's almost magical. You should make one to sell in the shop," Annie suggested. She knew Kate often sold her beautifully designed clothing in the shop. In fact, Annie had purchased a few pieces herself. Though the vest was probably a little too showy for her, she had to admit it was lovely and unexpected. "I am sure they'd sell easily."

"See? Annie agrees with me," Mary Beth told her blushing assistant. Then Mary Beth turned back to Annie. "As a reward for your support, I'll give you twenty percent off any last-minute gift kit." She gestured to a basket filled with small needlework kits that could be done in about an hour.

"Really?" Annie said in surprise. Mary Beth was a great friend but a shrewd shopkeeper.

"Oh, don't let her fool you," Kate said. She held up a white cardboard sign she'd been carefully lettering. It said, "Last-Minute Gift Kits—Now 20% Off!"

"You still can have the first discount," Mary Beth said grinning.

Annie poked through the basket. She picked up a cute kit for a plastic canvas shark with big googly eyes. When the cheeks of the shark were pinched, he opened his mouth. "Oh, John would love one of these," she said, imagining it tied on his Christmas package. "But I have no idea how to do this kind of embroidery."

"It's super easy," Mary Beth said. "I'll show you. You could learn it in minutes."

"OK then, you've made a sale!"

"I'll walk you through the steps for the embroidery right after the meeting," Mary Beth promised.

As Mary Beth rang up the little kit, the door opened with a rush of cold air that made Annie shiver. Gwendolyn Palmer and Stella Brickson came through the door together.

Always stylish, Gwen wore a gorgeous pair of chocolate brown wool slacks with a wool cape the color of cappuccino. The cape hung low in the front and back, and higher on the sides with a hem that reminded Annie of a man's dress shirt. It also had a two wool scarves attached—one scarf in the cappuccino color and the other in vanilla. Annie did notice that Gwen had traded in her normal pumps for low-heeled leather boots.

Looking at the perfectly put together outfit, Annie felt a little like a lumberjack in her long flannel tunic and fleecy knit pants with her snow boots. At least her heavy wool coat had a row of cute toggle fasteners.

"Now I know I'm late," Stella said when she caught sight of Annie. Normally Stella beat everyone to the club meetings. When Annie had first moved to Stony Point, she almost suspected Stella lived in the comfy chair at the shop. "We were held up. Some out-of-towner in a ridiculous rolling box had slid into a ditch."

"Oh, I hope no one was hurt," Annie said.

"It didn't appear so," Stella said. "When the officers finally waved us on, I saw the driver. She seemed fine, though dressed ridiculously for this weather."

"Not everyone can handle New England winters," Alice said gently.

Stella sniffed and Annie could practically hear the older woman's thoughts. Stella was very critical of tourists and newcomers to Stony Point. She was the self-appointed matriarch of the town, and so far, no one had the nerve to remind her that she'd only come back to Stony Point five years earlier than Annie. Stella had lived an elegant life in New York City until her husband died, and she returned to the town she considered her own, Stony Point.

"Peggy should be along in a minute," Gwen said as she pulled off a lovely pair of soft leather gloves. "I just came from the diner, and she was finishing up with a few customers. They've gotten really busy with all the ..."

"Shhhhhh!" Mary Beth interrupted. "Don't spill Peggy's secret. She'll never forgive you!"

"You've really got my curiosity going now," Annie said.

Stella pulled out a gorgeous piece of knitted fabric in an icy blue. Immediately her needles began the regular clicking that signified Stella was in the building. Annie suspected Stella could knit through a hurricane.

The other women began drifting toward their seats just

as the front door burst open with a bang. "Oh, sorry!" Peggy exclaimed as she hurried through and hauled the door shut behind her. "The wind caught it."

"That's all right," Mary Beth said. "It happens a lot this time of year. I'm just happy when the glass doesn't shatter."

"You mean it does sometimes?" Annie asked in surprise.

"Once," Mary Beth said. "But I'm always nervous of a repeat. The yarn gets very mobile when there's no glass in the door to keep out the wind."

Annie settled into her chair, her mind still on the amazing force nature seemed fond of displaying during the Maine winters. Her door at Grey Gables had blown open once or twice, scaring her half to death every time. She pulled the half-finished scarf from her project bag but didn't begin crocheting, she just stroked the soft yarn while she thought.

"So, is she going to do it?" Peggy Carson asked as she pulled her own project from her purse and laid it down in her lap. The earth tones of the beautifully pieced quilt block contrasted sharply with Peggy's pink waitress uniform.

"I haven't told her a thing about it," Alice said as she walked back to her seat. "You're the one who knows the most about it." Alice pulled her cross-stitch canvas out of her bag.

Stella Brickson glanced up at them, her knitting needles clicking softly. "I can't believe any of you are considering spending extra time outside in this weather."

Annie looked around, puzzled. "What exactly are we considering?"

"Being movie stars," Peggy said, her eyes dreamy. "A movie crew is coming to Stony Point this week!"

"This week?" Annie looked from one excited face to another. Only Mary Beth and Stella seemed their normal selves in the face of the news. "Isn't that kind of sudden?"

"They were going to film in Storm Harbor, but that last winter storm did some damage that would have ruined the shots," Peggy said. "Apparently they were in a panic to find a new location and our own Mayor Butler saved the day by offering the use of our waterfront."

Annie didn't bother to ask Peggy how she knew all this. As Peggy waited on tables at The Cup & Saucer, she sucked up information like a vacuum. There weren't many secrets in Stony Point that didn't get talked about in the diner. "OK, what does that have to do with becoming movie stars?"

"They're going to need extras," Peggy said. "They're having a casting call this afternoon for a scene down at the waterfront."

"Sounds cold," Stella said.

Annie had to agree. She got enough icy ocean breezes right in the front yard at Grey Gables. She had no interest in going any closer to the water. "I think I'll pass."

"You should come," Alice said. "I'm going, and so is Peggy."

"So am I!" A cheery voice called out as a long-legged teenage girl walked out of the back room and leaned on the front counter. Annie turned to smile at Kate Stevens's daughter, Vanessa.

"As long as it doesn't interfere with school," Kate reminded her.

"It won't. I'm sure they'll be long gone before break is over," Vanessa said. "Besides, I could always count it toward my career-planning days."

"What career would that be?" Kate asked, frowning.

"Acting, of course," Vanessa said, tossing her hair. "Don't you think I'd be a great actress?"

"I think you'll be great at whatever you decide to do," Mary Beth said fondly. It was clear the owner of A Stitch in Time doted on Vanessa like an affectionate aunt. Mary Beth had never married and had no children of her own, so she often mothered both Kate and Vanessa a bit.

"It still sounds cold," Annie said. "I'm going to sit this one out. You guys can shiver without me."

Naturally, Annie's friends couldn't just let her bow out. Annie could see the determination to talk her into it on several faces.

"The mayor will be there," Peggy said.

Annie felt her face flush as her friends grinned at her, and she steeled herself for more teasing about Mayor Ian Butler. Ian had made his fondness for Annie quite clear, but Annie was keeping it strictly friends between them. She'd already married, loved, and lost her beloved Wayne. After his passing, she really wasn't interested in romance, though she was glad Ian had become a good friend.

Of course, she had to admit her friends weren't totally coming out of left field with their teasing. She'd gone out with Ian a few times for engagements that could only be called dates. He'd talked her into going to a karaoke restaurant, and then he serenaded her from the stage. And she'd been his date for the formal Harvest Ball as well. Still, despite what those things might look like to the romance-obsessed Hook and Needle Club, she firmly considered Ian Butler to be a good friend—a really handsome, good friend.

"Are you sure you want to leave him out there in the cold all by himself?" Alice asked, her blue eyes sparkling.

"Especially around beautiful actresses," Gwen Palmer added, kiddingly.

"Oh?" Annie asked, hoping to change the subject. "Do you know who is going to be in the film?"

"No," Peggy said glumly. "But I hope Brad Pitt will be the star. I would love to see him in real life. Or Matt Damon. I just loved him in those *Bourne* movies. Wally and I have seen all of them."

"I've seen those too and all the *Ocean* movies. He's in those," Alice said, then grinned. "Though I like George Clooney better. Now there is an actor I'd love to see close up."

"Or Orlando Bloom," Gwen said.

"Gwendolyn Palmer! that boy is half your age!" Stella scolded, clearly scandalized.

"He is *not* half my age! Of course, my marriage is older than him," Gwen said. Annie saw a wicked sparkle in her eye. "I just like his acting, he's very talented. I admire talented people."

Stella just harrumphed, which sent all the women into giggles.

~ 2 ~

While the rest of the Hook and Needle Club laughed, Gwen kept naming young actors who all had work she admired. Finally Stella refused to react anymore, though the older woman's knitting needles still seemed to click disapprovingly.

"Really, Annie," Alice said when Gwen finally settled back with her own knitting and stopped teasing Stella. "You have to promise to think about it. It won't be nearly as much fun without you."

"What does this audition require?" Annie asked. "Will we have to wear costumes or memorize lines?"

Peggy shook her head. "We're just supposed to gather in the Community Center at four this afternoon. I've already gotten permission to take a long break at the diner." At that, her eyes suddenly widened and she looked down at her watch. "Speaking of which, I promised to be back by now. I have to run!" She gathered her things and did just that.

Stella sighed as they watched the pretty young waitress hurry out the door, trotting past the big front window on her way to the diner. "I wish she didn't have to work so hard," Stella said. "I've tried to give them money, you know. Then she wouldn't have to work so many hours. She and Wally wouldn't take it." Stella shook her head. "Too much pride."

Annie smiled a little at that. Pride was something Stella

herself had in great abundance. In fact, her pride had nearly made Annie's life miserable when she first came back to Stony Point after Betsy died. Annie was glad she could now see Stella's warm heart under her proud, prickly exterior.

"So, Annie," Alice said. "Are you going to join us this afternoon? Please?"

Annie frowned, and then laughed as Alice clasped her hands dramatically and turned on her most pitiful begging look. "I guess so, but I'm going to feel completely silly," Annie said finally. "And if I catch cold, you have to bring me some of your homemade chicken soup."

"I will," Alice agreed with a grin.

"Now, could we possibly spend some time on our projects?" Stella asked with a sniff. "Sometimes I do wonder if we've forgotten why we get together."

"I would never forget," Gwen said. "We do it for the gossip."

Everyone laughed except Stella, but Annie was fairly certain she'd seen a sparkle in the older woman's eyes before she dipped her head to stare intently at her knitting.

"I noticed your knitting when you came in," Annie said. "That pattern is beautiful. The cables have such an unusual twist. They remind me of vines."

Stella beamed at Annie. "I thought so too. In fact, I was going to ask Alice for a favor."

"Me?" Alice said, surprised. "I don't know anything about knitting."

"But you do beautiful embroidery," Stella said. "I was wondering if you would considering putting some silk roses on this dress when it's done."

Stella pointed out where she would like to see roses blooming, near the neckline and then along the patterned hem of the dress. "I know it would be a considerable amount of work, and I would definitely want to compensate you," she said.

"I wasn't worried about that," Alice said. "I'm just not sure I'm good enough at silk ribbon embroidery. I still consider myself a bit of a newcomer to it. When will you be ready for me to do it?"

"Oh, probably not for another month," Stella said. "This pattern is very involved, and it's only one of the projects I'm working on."

"OK," Alice said. "I'll do some practice projects before then and make sure I'm capable."

"That's a beautiful scarf," Kate said, lifting the edge of Annie's crocheting. "I love that shade of pink."

"It's for my granddaughter," Annie said. "She's fallen in love with some book character who only wears pink. So I thought this fluffy pink yarn would make her a perfect scarf."

"Does anyone even need a scarf in Texas?" Vanessa asked as she stepped into the group and sat next to her mother in Peggy's vacated chair. Vanessa sometimes took part in different needlecrafts through the teen group the Hook and Needle Club had started.

"Only about one month a year," Annie admitted. "But she can wear it when she visits me here too."

"Are they coming up for Christmas?" Mary Beth asked.

Annie sighed. "Not this year, and I'm not going there either. The airfares are simply out of our league. Right now we're hoping to make a nice long visit when the children are out of school for the summer. Something long enough to justify the cost of getting here."

"I hate flying at Christmas," Alice said. "The weather up here makes every flight more of a hope than a sure thing. And the crowds!" She shuddered and picked up her cross-stitch.

"So you're not flying off for some romantic rendezvous with a certain dashing photographer?" Gwen asked.

"I'm not even flying off for a painful rendezvous with a certain crabby mother in Florida," Alice said with a laugh. "You guys are stuck with me for Christmas."

"We should do something together," Annie said. "We should have a party."

"We could have it here if you want," Mary Beth said. "I'm stuck here for Christmas too. My sister and niece are going to Europe for Christmas. It's magazine business for Melanie, but I do think she's trying to unbend a little and build some bridges with Amy."

"I have to bow out," Gwen said. "Christmas is always crazy for us. It seems like John does a million networking things over the holidays." She sighed. "It's why I was hoping for a little vicarious romance. How about you, Annie? Are you and Ian doing anything?"

Annie felt her face grow warm. "Not as far as I know," she said. "The mayor doesn't plan his calendar around me."

"Of course not," Alice agreed solemnly, and the group laughed again. Just when Annie thought the heat in her cheeks was ready to ignite, Kate asked her another question about her crocheting, and the conversation shifted again.

The rest of the meeting passed quickly. As Annie folded the fluffy pink scarf carefully around the crochet hook, she marveled at how quickly meetings passed now. She'd sat through more than one coldly awkward meeting when she'd first come to live at Grey Gables. She had wondered if she'd ever fit in the small community. Now she couldn't imagine life without the warm friendships of the Hook and Needle Club.

Before she left the snug little shop, Annie opened the cute plastic canvas shark kit, and Mary Beth got her started on the stitches she needed. The shop owner had been right. It was easy, and she had the first piece of the shark mostly done before she stuffed the little kit in her project bag and headed back out into the cold.

After the meeting, Annie gingerly crossed the street so she could stare into store windows. She still had a list of last-minute Christmas presents, mostly for the people she could never buy well for. LeeAnn's husband, Herb, was on the list. In the past, she'd bought him a tie, socks, a sweatshirt representing his favorite college basketball team, and even a special golf glove LeeAnn had once suggested. Each gift was greeted with the same polite smile and thanks.

Annie peered into the window of the hardware store and wondered if Herb would like some kind of tool. LeeAnn told her that he was trying to be a little handier around the house.

The thought made Annie smile. Her own dear husband, Wayne, had loved the idea of being handy as well, even though he never advanced much beyond shelf-building and even those weren't always exactly level. But he never gave up trying, and he never stopped buying tools. A quick glance at their garage in Texas would have made anyone think Wayne was a master woodworker with all the tools he had, each neatly in its own spot.

But would Herb have the same fascination with random tools?

"Now, what could the hardware store possibly have done to bring on that frown?" asked a deep voice said from behind her.

Annie turned to smile up at Ian Butler. With Wayne so fresh in her mind, Annie once again thought of the two men as if they were side by side. Both were tall, but Wayne had always kept the solid build that hinted at his football-playing days in college. Ian was slighter, but still a strong man with an easy self-confidence. Like Wayne, Ian could make her feel safe whenever he was around. He was a good friend that way; she could count on him.

She noticed the mayor had chosen to dress for warmth over formality today. The cold wind always made her earlobes ache, so she couldn't blame anyone for piling on the layers. The thick fisherman knit sweater that peeked out from under Ian's peacoat looked cozy warm.

"I'm just trying to decide on a present for my son-in-law," Annie said.

"At a hardware store?" Ian said.

"I'm a desperate woman." She told him about the weak success of all of her past gifts.

"Not even a grin for the golf glove?"

Annie shook her head.

"That is a tough case," Ian agreed. "What kinds of things does he like?"

"Work, my daughter, the kids," Annie said, ticking them

off on her fingers. Then she paused, and finally added, "He seems fond of his car."

"I sense you two haven't truly bonded."

"No, that's not it. He's a really lovely person and a great husband. He's just kind of quiet and thoughtful."

Ian was quiet for a moment, his face pensive. "Does he read? Maybe he would like a book?" Ian asked. "I spend a lot of evenings sharing a chair with Tartan while I read a good book."

"Actually, I think he does like to read. That's something he has in common with LeeAnn," Annie said. "But books are so personal. I'd have no idea how to choose." She turned to look into the hardware store window again, and then turned away. There were clearly no answers there.

She smiled up at Ian as an idea struck her. "Are you really going to be in the movie they're filming here?"

"Not in any noticeable way," Ian said, "but if I'm asking my constituents to consider standing out in the cold for the sake of promoting the town, I thought I should too. I'll be some background extra shivering in the icy cold like every-one else. Then when the movie comes out, I'll be able to say, 'See that elbow shaking in the far corner of the screen? That's me!'"

Annie smiled. "Glad to hear you're not going Hollywood on us."

"Not me. I will, of course, need my own dressing room. And I'll have to insist they shoot only my good side," he said with mock seriousness. "So, which do you think is my good side?" He turned to show her each profile.

Annie smiled. "I think you're safe either way, Mr. Mayor."

"Do the questions mean you're going to be an extra too?" he asked.

"Well, maybe," she said. "It's become a minor obsession with some of the Hook and Needle Club. Still, I can't imagine that they'll need everyone, so maybe they'll skip me, and I'll get to stay home."

"Don't count on it. I think they need as much crowd as they can get," Ian said. "I don't know how eager people are going to be to stand out in the cold—even for a movie. Also, since this is last minute, I don't know how many people have even heard about it."

Annie laughed. "If they haven't heard about it, it wasn't Peggy Carson's fault. I certainly hope they let her be an extra. She will be heartbroken if they don't. She's so excited about the movie that I'm sure she's told everyone who comes to the diner."

"And that would be just about everyone in Stony Point," Ian agreed. "Speaking of which, would you like to grab some hot cocoa with me?"

"I'll have to ask for a rain check," Annie said. "Or maybe a snow check. I'm going to head for home and work on some of my Christmas projects."

"Good for you," Ian said. "But I'll see you this afternoon at the casting call?"

"Unless I chicken out before then."

"The fearless Annie Dawson?" Ian said in mock shock. "I could not imagine it. I'll definitely see you there."

Annie smiled fondly after Ian as he walked across the street with the same long-legged stride he'd use in the summer. He never seemed to have any trouble with the ice and snow. She didn't know if he just had really great boots, or if he somehow defied gravity.

She turned back and gave the hardware store one last wistful glance. Tools definitely weren't the answer for Herb's gift. She'd have to keep working on that. She carefully walked back to her car and headed for home. As she drove, the sun peeked out from the ridged snow clouds now and then, just enough to keep her hopeful.

She pulled up in front of the tall Victorian house that she'd inherited from her grandmother. When Annie had first come to claim the house, she wasn't sure she wanted it. Her grandmother's illness had been worse than she'd ever shared with Annie. And Annie had been too grief stricken over Wayne's death to pay enough attention to anyone or anything else. As a result, Grey Gables had slipped into decline, and Annie hadn't even known.

But she'd found the perfect handyman in Peggy's husband, Wally. He'd done wonders with the place. Now, as she looked up at the house, she saw each individual project: new paint, new gingerbread trim, repairs to the porch rail and steps. It had all seemed so overwhelming, and now those very projects helped make it feel very much like home.

The snow covering the yard had the sparkle of an icy crust over the top. Annie liked the peaceful beauty of snow, but she missed her flowers too. "Oh well," she said softly. "Spring will be here before I know it." Then she shook her head ruefully at her own behavior. Talking to herself. Now all she had to do was adopt about twenty more cats, and she officially could be an odd widow lady.

She stepped out of the car and gasped again as the wind

off the ocean tried to freeze the breath right in her lungs. She fought the urge to run for the house, a few sprawls on the icy porch steps during the first winter in Maine had cured her of undue haste.

Finally she was inside, with the door closed tightly against winter, and a warm cat making demanding sounds at her feet. She scooped up Boots and held her close to her chilled face. Boots wriggled for a moment, then settled against her and purred.

Annie carried Boots into the kitchen and rewarded her face warming with a small bit of cat kibble.

"I can't believe I agreed to go back out in this weather for something as silly as being in a movie," Annie said aloud.

Boots glanced up at her from the bowl and offered a questioning meow.

Annie laughed. "I guess you don't know why I would do it either. Well, on the upside, at least there's no mystery about it. I know I'm going to freeze to death."

~3~

Annie pulled open the Community Center door and smiled at the warmth that flowed out. That was one of her favorite things about winter. Every time she stepped indoors somewhere, it was like getting a warm hug from the building.

Just inside the door, several cheerful teens stood holding piles of clipboards. Annie recognized two of them from the unfortunate mum school fundraiser when she'd ended up buying so many pots of mums she couldn't get on her front porch until Ian had found someone to take them off her hands.

"Hi, Mrs. Dawson!" A grinning red-haired boy named Jeremy handed her a clipboard. Jeremy had sold mums to her too, but she forgave him since he was the shoveling angel who kept the driveway and porch clear at Grey Gables. Without him, Annie would just have to huddle inside until spring like a groundhog. "You're supposed to fill this out," Jeremy said.

"Thank you, Jeremy. And thank you for the last shoveling. You must get out in the middle of the night."

Jeremy shrugged. "I have several houses I clear," he said. "I don't want anyone to slip and fall because they had to go out before I got around to them. Besides," he grinned, "you guys pay great."

"And it's worth every penny," Annie said. Her eyes swept over the form, and then she nodded and walked on, looking around the room.

The Community Center was mostly one huge room. At one end of the long room, a small kitchenette was separated from the rest of the space by a half-wall topped with a counter. The rest of that end of the building was taken up with two small restrooms. The other end of the building held a small stage.

When the Community Center was used for classes, temporary walls were pulled on ceiling tracks to separate the one large room into two smaller ones. Today the canvas-covered walls were folded back neatly. Rows of chairs filled most of the large space, and Annie spotted a number of people she knew who were already seated.

Vanessa and her best friend Mackenzie turned just then and waved at Annie, which triggered waving from several others. Annie smiled. It was nice to feel like part of the community.

She continued to scan the crowd for Alice's auburn hair and spotted her friend in one of the front rows. She was glad to see an empty seat beside Alice and headed to it. "Nice crowd," she said as she slipped into the seat.

Alice looked around. "Peggy seems to have done a great job of spreading the word. The movie crew should hire her to do all their advance publicity."

"I didn't see Peggy in the crowd," Annie said. "Has she made it?"

"Not yet," Alice said. "But you know her boss. He won't let her go from the diner until the last possible second.

Peggy's his best waitress."

Annie nodded. "I just hope she makes it. She was so excited. She'd wilt like a lily in the desert if she didn't get to take part."

Annie twisted in her seat to look over the crowd again. Vanessa gave her another big smile before leaning close to whisper something to Mackenzie. The two girls reminded Annie a bit of her and Alice. They tended to get into a lot more trouble together than they ever did alone, but they enjoyed every second of it.

Then she spotted Peggy hurrying in the front door, her thick coat hanging loose over her waitress uniform. Annie sighed in relief as she turned back around. "Peggy made it!"

"And just in time." Alice nodded toward the stage.

A young woman in a crisp, well-tailored suit and heels briskly climbed the steps up to the stage, followed by two men. One of the men was Ian, but the other was a complete stranger.

Annie would have bet the young woman and Peggy were the only two women in the room who weren't in their warmest possible pants. Annie suddenly wondered if this was the woman Stella had seen stuck in a snowbank off the road. This time of year, that neat suit and heels definitely would have qualified as being dressed ridiculously.

The woman walked to the middle of the stage and tapped the microphone, producing the soft thump that proved the microphone was on. She unseated it from the stand and spoke. "Thank you all for coming out on such short notice. I am Kathleen Kensington, the casting agent. I'll be choosing who will take part in the movie. We have need for two different crowd scenes, so most, if not all of you will be invited to take part. We pay a hundred dollars a day."

The crowd began to murmur, and Annie knew the prospect of getting a hundred dollars for something that they would have done for free was welcome news. Kathleen Kensington waited patiently for the room to quiet.

"Please fill out the form you were given at the door," Ms. Kensington said. "If anyone missed getting a form, please raise your hand, and we'll get you one right now." A few hands came up, and the young woman waited until those people had their clipboards.

"After you finish filling out the form, just turn it in at the door on your way out," Ms Kensington said. "We'll get back to you by tomorrow about whether we'll need you for the film. If you have an email address, we'll email. Otherwise, we'll call. Our first day of shooting will be Thursday."

People began to shuffle in their seats a bit, and Ms. Kensington held up her hand to indicate she wasn't finished. "I also want to thank Mayor Butler for allowing us to come to Stony Point and film *A Very Maine Christmas*. He really saved us from a difficult spot." Ms. Kensington spoke her thanks in the same brisk cool tone as every other remark.

The crowd clapped politely for Ian, and he bowed with a sparkling grin.

"I have one other person who would like to speak to you," Ms. Kensington said as the applause died off. "This is our prop master Samuel Ely."

A young man stepped up to the microphone and pushed his wire-rim glasses up his nose. He was long-legged and thin, giving him the gangly look of a boy who had not yet filled out. "I have a favor to ask of you," he said. "Our first scene will be a ferry unloading passengers, so some of you will be coming off the ferry, and some will be greeting it. Those coming off will need to be holding small suitcases. Since this scene was a last-minute addition, I'm looking for older suitcases from at least the 1950s. I have picked up a number of workable pieces of luggage from local thrift stores, but if you could check your attics for any older pieces, there will be an extra pay of twenty dollars a day for any cases you can let us borrow."

Alice poked Annie gently. "A trip to the attic!"

"I will be staying at Maplehurst Inn," he said. "If you find a case and want to know if it will work for the film, simply bring it by the inn and show it to me. You can be paid for the use of your luggage even if you aren't in the scene on Thursday. If you are in the scene, you can simply bring your luggage then, and someone in wardrobe will tell you then whether it will work."

He turned then and walked to a small pile of suitcases near the curtain. He picked up several and carried them back to the mike. "These are the sort of pieces we're looking for." He held them up one by one. They were all small—more overnight bags than full-sized luggage. Some were covered in canvas and some in leather. One tattered black case was plastered with travel stickers. "If you find pieces like this, please be sure to bring them."

The young man stepped back and let Kathleen Kensington finish up, thanking the group again for coming out and repeating her directions about the form. Annie took the pen from the clip and began filling out her form.

She frowned over questions about her height and weight, but she guessed that sort of thing was important to movie makers.

"It's a good thing Stella decided not to take part," Alice whispered. "She would blow a gasket over this form."

Annie smiled. "The age question alone would bring on a rant, I expect."

"You know it." Alice bumped shoulders playfully with Annie. "I'm glad you're taking part in this. We'll have fun."

"We'll freeze!" Annie said, and then she smiled. "But in the most enjoyable way, I'm sure."

"So," Alice said as she finished up her form, "when shall we search Betsy's attic for luggage? You've seen my attic at the carriage house. There's one steamer trunk and that's about it for luggage. No one has the kind of stash Betsy did."

Annie smiled. Her grandmother Betsy Holden had never thrown away anything she considered valuable. And Betsy's kind heart and loyalty meant she ended up storing more than a few things for others as well. The attic of Grey Gables was crammed with years of memories—and more than a few mysteries. Annie definitely remembered having seen some small suitcases up there. "We'll take a look whenever you want," she said.

"Let's do it early tomorrow morning," Alice said. "I'll bring over something good for breakfast, and then we'll head up to the attic."

"You know I'm always in favor of Alice MacFarlane's baked goods," Annie said. "I think that's a great idea. But not too early; I don't want you falling. Wait until the sun is bright enough to melt the icy patches."

Alice laughed. "That might be spring." Then she held up a hand as Annie started to comment. "No, I know what you mean. I'll be over after nine; does that sound OK?"

"That would be just perfect."

Annie and Alice stood and moved toward the door. It was a slow process since the excited crowd kept stopping to form small groups and chatter. More than once, someone tugged on Annie's arm to whisper, "Isn't this amazing?"

Finally, they handed in their clipboards. They stepped out into the icy wind and gasped at the cold. "Whew! Every time I do this today, I wonder why I'm going along with the movie idea," Annie said.

Alice grinned as she wrapped her long scarf tighter around her neck. "You're doing it for the adventure."

"Right. Adventure."

"Oh, you might as well admit it," Alice said. "You like adventure as much as I do. And I think you're even more curious. You'd be miserable if you were left out."

"Probably," Annie admitted. "See you in the morning."

The two women hurried through the parking lot separately. Annie was glad her car heater warmed up quickly. By the time she pulled out of the lot, she could already feel her fingers again. She had a fleeting hope that she simply wouldn't be picked to be in the movie. But then she had to admit that Alice was right. She really wouldn't want to miss finding out what it was like to be a movie extra. And she did wonder a bit about which actors might be in the film.

Annie spent the rest of the day cozy at home. She finished Joanna's scarf and the cute little shark for John. She slipped a wrapped candy into the shark's closed mouth, and then tied him on the outside of the package she'd already wrapped for John. She'd found him a perfect captain's hat in his size and knew he would be crazy about it.

Annie laid the pink fluffy scarf in a bed of white tissue embedded with pink sequins inside a long box. Then she wrapped the present and put both of the gifts into the larger shipping box along with LeeAnn's present.

Annie had spent months on the crocheted coverlet for LeeAnn. It was a simple granny square pattern done in black yarn with jewel-tone centers. The result had been striking and Annie knew it would be a perfect complement for the daring colors LeeAnn had used to decorate their home. Annie only wished she had a gift idea that matched as perfectly for Herb. She made a mental note to ask LeeAnn about Herb's taste in books.

Annie looked back down at the mostly filled shipping box. She wondered if she should go ahead and seal the box so she could get it in the mail. She could always ship Herb's separately. At the rate she was going, at least LeeAnn and the kids would have their gifts on time. Annie dashed off a quick note about Herb's present being in a separate package. Then she added a tin of Christmas cookies she'd baked for the twins and sealed the box. She'd go out to the post office later.

Sighing, Annie decided to spend a while crocheting the lovely filet crochet table runner she had been working on for weeks. The dresser in the upstairs guest room was a beautiful antique piece that was a bit battered on top. It would look gorgeous with the runner draped across it. Annie had charted the crocket design herself, basing it on the pattern in the window drapes. She was very proud of the detail, but it required total concentration, so she would probably still be working on it well into the spring.

The evening passed quickly as Annie slipped into the zone with her crocheting. It wasn't until Boots jumped into her lap with a chorus of demanding meows that she realized it had grown late. Annie put away her project carefully, remembering to put the project bag in a cupboard away from curious cat paws. Then she carried Boots off to bed with the comfortable feeling of a day well spent.

As she walked down the hall, she paused to turn down the thermostat. As much as Annie didn't enjoy being cold, she loved that winter let her pile quilts on her bed for sleeping. As Annie snuggled under the handmade quilts from Betsy Holden's collection, she always felt close to her grandmother.

Betsy had loved beautiful things, but even more than that, she had loved things made by hand. "When someone creates something with her hands," Betsy had told her, "with each stitch she sews part of herself into every piece. The same goes for knitting or crocheting. Everything you make will have a bit of you in it. And when you pass it on, you make connections from your heart."

Betsy had certainly made many connections with her own handwork. Though Annie's grandmother loved trying many crafts, the one she was really known for was cross-stitch. She created worlds with her needle, and those worlds had lived on. "Proving that Gram was right," Annie told the sleepy cat in her arms.

Wednesday dawned clear and bright. The morning sun

on the snow was nearly dazzling as Annie looked out. She hoped this weather would settle in for as long as the film crew was in town. Not only would it be more comfortable, it was just safer, especially since they were going to be filming around the water. Ian had told her how treacherous the waterfront piers got in icy conditions.

Annie made a full pot of coffee to welcome Alice. She stood at the front windows sipping from her favorite mug and watching for her friend. Soon she spotted Alice crossing the yard.   Alice lived in what had once been the carriage house for Grey Gables, back in the days when both properties belonged to just one family.

Alice carried a basket covered in tea towels, and Annie's stomach growled in anticipation. Alice's goodies were always fantastic. Annie fully believed her friend could make a living with her baking if she wanted to, but Alice preferred selling Princessa jewelry and Divine Décor items at home parties. Baking was Alice's play, and she didn't want to rob it of any of the fun by making it a job.

Annie had the door open by the time Alice reached the top of the porch steps. As her friend stomped snow from her boots on the mat, Annie took the basket. Boots sniffed the air through the door, but it was too cold for the cat to be interested in dashing outside.

"Ready for an attic adventure?" Alice asked as she came in and slipped out of her long wool coat. The forest green sweatshirt she wore underneath made Annie laugh out loud. Alice had cross-stitched "Attic Adventurer" across the front along with images of piles of trunks and hatboxes.

"Oh, that is wonderful," Annie said. "When did you make it?"

"About a month ago," Alice said grinning. "You cannot imagine how itchy I've been to have a reason to wear it."

"Today's the day," Annie said. "But only after spending some time with whatever is in this basket. You have me trained. I practically drool whenever I see you carrying a basket my way."

Alice laughed. "This is drool-worthy stuff—zucchini and blueberry bread. I froze bags of blueberries and shredded zucchini last summer just so I could make this to remind me of summer in the dreary winter. It's even healthy!"

They walked back to the kitchen and settled down at the small table near the window with fresh mugs of coffee and thick slices of warm bread. "How has the attic organization been going?" Alice said.

"It's on hold again," Annie said. "I need to bring down at least a few Christmas decorations. It's hard to get excited about decorating without LeeAnn and the kids here. I keep putting it off."

"I always do a few things," Alice said. "I like candles in the windows and wreaths. Then I put out the crèche on the fireplace mantel. I don't always do a tree, though when I don't, I usually wish I had. I love the smell of pine in the house. Every year I think I'm not going to do much, but then I add and add more decorations as Christmas gets closer."

"I thought I would pass on a tree this year," Annie said. "It just gives Boots new ways to make mischief." Then she paused and laughed a little. "Listen to me. I sound a little Scrooge-like."

"I don't think you could be like Scrooge if you tried," Alice said. "So should we poke around for Christmas decorations while we're up there today?"

Annie waved a hand. "No, no poking. We're going to

grab the suitcases and get out before a mystery tackles us. With the movie and Christmas gifts to find, I have enough to do. No mysteries."

Alice just shook her head smiling. "I think I've heard that before. Usually just before a really juicy plot unfolds."

Annie moaned, because she knew Alice was right about that. Surely the mysteries would give her time off for Christmas. Wouldn't they?

After chatting a bit about Christmas projects, Alice took a last gulp of her coffee and stood up. "I'm ready for the attic challenge," she said. She took a dramatic stance. "To the attic!"

Annie turned a longing glance at the rest of the warm loaf of bread on the counter, but decided her waistline would be better off if they went ahead and began the hunt. She laughed and echoed. "To the attic! Back off, mysteries; we're on our way!"

4

When the women reached the attic, Alice looked around approvingly. "Every time we come up here, it looks a little more organized," she said. "Betsy would be so impressed."

Though the attic still held an amazing array of all sorts of things, many were now in boxes or plastic bins with clear labels. Even several of the large steamer trunks now had tags hanging from them with a general list of the contents.

"I actually piled up a lot of small suitcases over here," Annie said, slipping through the neat rows of trunks and boxes. "I saw this cute coffee table in a decorator magazine. It was made from old suitcases and small trunks with a top made from distressed wood. I thought it was wonderful. After Christmas, I'm going to show it to Wally to see if he could make one for me." Annie stopped at a large stack of luggage. "As you can see, I probably have a few cases to spare."

"Are they all empty?" Alice asked.

"I don't know," Annie said. "I haven't opened all of them."

She looked over the pile and picked up a small leather-covered valise. The corners of the suitcase were capped with silver to protect them from bumps. Annie liked the different shades of brown in the leather. The large sides of the case were clad in a smooth milk chocolate-color leather while the edges were bound in caramel-color strips. Each of the short sides of the case was covered in leather the color of dark chocolate. The end result was almost mouthwatering.

"That's a nice one," Alice said. "You know, I think one of the cases that the prop master held up looked a lot like that one. I remember thinking it looked like a candy shop."

"Well, then we know this one will work," Annie said. "Which one do you like?"

Alice rooted a bit, and then pulled out a small case covered in horsehair canvas and trimmed in reddish leather. "I think this is Hermes," she said, examining the hardware closely. "Look at the engraving on the metal. It looks like it was done by hand. I'll bring this one."

"Hermes?" Annie said. "Is that valuable?"

"It's designer and seems to be in nice shape," Alice said, "but I don't think it's particularly valuable. Unless, of course, it contains a stash of cash or diamonds."

Annie shook her finger. "Don't talk like that," she said. "You never know what we might find."

Alice flipped the latches and opened the case. A creamy linen-covered tray fit down into the case with elastic straps running the length of the tray to catch small items you might not want rattling around in the suitcase. Nothing lay in the tray, but once they lifted it out, they saw a small bundle of sepia-toned photos tied in a ribbon. "No diamonds," Alice said as she took the bundle from the case. "Just someone's photos."

Annie took the bundle and gently untied the ribbon. "Oh, I recognize these," she said as she leafed through them. "They belonged to my grandfather. Look, that's him in his uniform." She held the photos out for Alice to see. Her grandfather stood very erect; he looked so young and dashing. She felt a pang of melancholy that she couldn't carry the bundle to her grandfather and have him tell the story behind each one. She had always loved hearing him tell stories. "My grandfather loved photos. I saw another bundle like this in Gram's room. I'll put these in with them."

"All right," Alice said, "now you open your case. Maybe you got the diamonds."

Alice set her case down and held her breath as Annie snapped it open. The inside was completely empty. "Ah-ha, no mystery here!" Annie exclaimed. "Just an empty box."

"Oh well, I guess we can't score a juicy mystery every time we come to the attic," Alice said with a mock pout. "I think we should console ourselves with some more zucchini bread."

"That sounds good." Annie looked over the pile of luggage. "Do you think we should take another case, just to help out? That young man seemed anxious to get enough."

"Oh, tempting fate," Alice said, with a grin. "I'm game. I would cheerfully open them all. With your history in this attic, we'd be sure to find a mystery in one of them! Are you sure you want to open another one?"

Annie pulled another case from the pile. This small, hard-sided valise was covered in printed fabric. The background was charcoal gray with a small fleur-de-lis print. It was a pretty case, though faded. Annie liked the feminine quality it had. Her hand rested on the brass locks for a moment, and then she put it carefully back in the pile. "Let's not tempt fate," she said. "I think some zucchini bread is a better idea."

"Well, I would love to find a mystery, but eating sounds like a great backup plan," Alice said, shrugging good-naturedly.

They hurried downstairs to cut a slice while the loaf was still warm.

Annie smiled as she looked back at the attic. Somehow it seemed like a victory to get out of the attic with nothing that anyone could possibly consider mysterious.

They snacked on bread for a while, and Annie asked how the Divine Décor business was going.

"When the tourists leave, I always have a bit of a lull," Alice said, and then waved a hand in the direction of the window. "No one wants to go to any parties in this kind of weather. But it never completely dries up. My customers like to give little knickknacks for Christmas. In fact, my sister asked me to send her a couple things just last week. Which reminds me, I need to go package it up and run to the post office."

Annie brightened. "Would you mind taking a package for me? I finished Joanna's scarf last night, and I have the package all set to go to Texas. I have to admit, I was hoping to avoid going out in the snow at all today."

"I'll be glad to take it," Alice said, "but you have to be careful. You don't want to turn into a winter hermit. We have some folks in town who disappear into their nests all winter."

Annie laughed, since that was very close to what she'd been thinking about herself earlier. "I don't think you would let me be too much of a hermit," she said.

"I'm just returning the favor," Alice said. "You brought me out of my shell when you came home to take over Grey Gables. The least I can do is keep you from turning hermit."

Annie smiled. She still found it hard to believe her vivacious friend had withdrawn so much after her divorce, but all the Hook and Needle Club had confirmed it. Now Alice was one of the most outgoing people in Stony Point.

Annie gratefully got the box. As she carried it out of her room, she looked at Alice fretfully. "It's kind of heavy," she said. "I'm not sure you should carry it in the snow."

"Don't worry, I have experience with snow." Alice grabbed the box as if it were empty and headed on her way. Annie peeked through the curtains, following her friend's progress back to the carriage house, just to be sure she got there safely.

Sighing, she turned to Boots, who had come to rub against her ankle while she watched. "It looks like I'm the only person in Stony Point who doesn't know how to handle the snow."

Boots purred agreeably, and Annie scooped up the cat as she decided on what to do with the rest of her cozy day at home. She was halfway across the room when the phone rang. She dumped Boots gently on the sofa and snagged the phone.

"Mrs. Dawson?" a brisk female voice asked.

"This is she."

"This is Kathleen Kensington. I'm calling to say we would like you to be on set in the morning at 6:30. You won't need to wear anything special as wardrobe will outfit you. It might be good to plan your clothing around ease of removal since you will be changing quickly. Wear your hair loose if possible to make it easier for hair and makeup."

The voice paused, as if checking a list and Annie was able to squeeze in a question. "Where will the set be?"

"Down on Grand Avenue," Ms. Kensington said. "At the harbor. We'll be setting up tents and trailers to use for our staff, so it should be easy to spot from the street. We'll be the place that is very well lit."

Annie shivered at the thought of heading out while it was still dark. That definitely would be scary driving. Then scary driving made her think of Stella's story of the car driving off the road. "Ms. Kensington, were you in an auto mishap yesterday morning? Someone told me a car went off the road."

Ms. Kensington made a disgusted sound. "Yes, that was me. Well, actually ... Samuel and me. Someone ran us completely off the road. On these narrow roads, you would expect a little more courtesy."

"I hope you weren't injured," Annie said.

"No, nothing like that," the woman said, and then she sighed. "But my Jimmy Choos were completely ruined. I wish I had been driving. I'm originally from Minnesota. I handle snow better, though we don't normally run visitors off the road there."

"I assure you, we don't do that around here either," Annie said consolingly. "I'm originally from Texas, and I've found people here to be very kind. I'm sorry you had such an unpleasant first encounter. I hope Samuel wasn't injured?"

"No, we were both fine. I expect Samuel's rental-car company will be disgruntled about the scraped paint, but that's not really my worry. Thank you for your concern though. We'll see you on set in the morning."

With that, the woman quickly hung up the phone. Well, that's one mystery solved, Annie thought. She placed the phone gently in the cradle and looked around her cheerful front room. A little light housecleaning seemed in order, so she set about to do it.

By bedtime, Annie had the wood floors glowing and every speck of dust captured and removed. She liked keeping a clean, tidy house, though sometimes the ease of doing so made her feel a little nostalgic for the days when Wayne would forget to wipe his feet and track up her newly mopped kitchen floor. Or the years when LeeAnn was like a force of nature, carrying in collections of rocks, brightly colored leaves and even the occasional small creature.

Annie laughed to herself. No one would guess now, looking at the fashionable, self-assured woman that LeeAnn had grown up to be. Sometimes Annie looked at her daughter and tried to find some glimpse of the wild child she had once been. Usually she found it in the quirk of LeeAnn's smile or the occasional flash of her temper. Then, with that warm smile of nostalgia on her face, Annie ended her quiet day at home.

The morning of the filming started well before dawn. Annie groaned as the alarm clock beeped insistently in her ear. Boots shifted and stretched from her usual place on the bed, and then snuggled against the small of Annie's back like a purring heating pad.

Annie reached out and swatted at the clock until it fell silent. "Why did I agree to this?" she asked Boots.

The chubby cat didn't even bother to meow and merely curled herself up tightly as Annie sat up and felt around on the floor with her toes until she found her slippers. When Ms. Kensington had told her that everyone needed to be on set by 6:30 in the morning, Annie had almost said no, but then she imagined Alice giving her the big puppy eyes again. She didn't want to disappoint her friends.

"Why am I a pushover for everyone?" Annie moaned.

Boots looked up at her and sneezed.

"I agree," Annie said. "It's a sickness."

She shuffled to the closet and dressed as warmly as she could, starting with her silk long johns. Alice had called to offer to carpool so Annie wouldn't have to drive in the scary snow, but Annie wanted to take her own car. Now as she peered out the window at the dark morning sky, she wondered if she'd made a mistake. Alice was a much more confident driver in this kind of weather.

She headed to the kitchen to make a pot of coffee for her thermos. If she had to go out in the cold, she'd at least bring something hot to drink. Finally, she couldn't put it off any longer, and she headed out into the dark cold morning. It was every bit as unpleasant as she'd expected, but she took a moment to appreciate the stars still shining in the clear night sky. At least it wasn't likely to snow with the sky so clear.

The sky looked like a smooth black blanket scattered with bits of fairy dust. There were so many stars. Their home in Texas had security lights that came on anytime Annie stepped outside, and her neighbors all had their night lights on too. All that light pollution pushed back the fearfulness of night, but it drove away some of the wonder too. She never saw so many stars when she had looked up into the sky there.

A howl of wind rushed through the trees in the yard and made Annie jump. It was far too cold outside for more of her woolgathering—not unless she was going to find a way to wrap all that wool around herself for warmth.

Annie made the drive to the waterfront carefully. Sometimes the roads got icy at night after a bit of sun melt during the day. She was surprised at how brightly lit the pier was; Ms. Kensington wasn't kidding about that. You definitely couldn't miss the spectacle that the film crew made. A large crowd of people stood in huddled clumps under huge lights.

Annie grabbed her two suitcases and the thermos, and headed out. The wind was frigid but the huge lamps gave off more heat than she expected. They were almost blinding to look toward, but they were certainly nice to stand near for the warmth.

Annie spotted Alice and slipped through the crowd to reach her friend.

"You made it," Alice said with a grin. "They're taking people in groups into the wardrobe trailers to get dressed and made up."

"I hope we'll at least get to wear something warm," Annie echoed. Surely if they wanted a movie filmed in winter, they would have all the extras dress for the weather. She tried to imagine what kind of clothes they might be given. If they wanted old luggage, they probably were filming a period movie of some sort. Then she thought of how rarely women wore pants back in the nineteen fifties and before. The thought of changing into a skirt and standing where the wind could slip up her legs made Annie shiver even more. "Have you seen the clothes?"

Alice pointed and Annie saw a group that had already been in wardrobe and were now standing under a canvas tent. Big heaters were set up near the tent to keep the group warm. Annie noted right away that the women clearly wore dresses or skirts under the long coats.

"Look on the bright side," Alice said, giving her a supportive shoulder bump. "We get to stand in the warm spot after we're dressed. Think how glamorous we'll look in those costumes. We're apparently going to be well-off people from the early fifties."

Just then the wind rushed by, moaning between the trailers and tents. Annie felt like moaning along with it. Still, she told herself cheerfully, at least there aren't any mysteries here. Just goose bumps!

～5～

*I*n a few minutes, the casting director came by and beck-
oned Annie and Alice toward the wardrobe trailer along
with most of the people standing near them. Then the
woman led them to the trailer and spoke to each person at
the door.

As Alice stepped up to take her turn, Ms.
Kensington looked at Alice's beautiful auburn hair and said,
"Tell wardrobe that you're a greeter and that they absolutely
must not put a hat on you. You won't need the suitcase. Do
you mind if someone else carries it?"

"I don't mind," Alice turned to look at Annie. "Is that
all right?"

"Of course," Annie said.

"Wardrobe will tag it so it gets back to you, and so you
get paid for bringing the case," Ms. Kensington said.

Alice climbed the two metal steps and entered the trailer.
Annie stepped up to take her place. "Tell them you're going
on the ferry," Ms. Kensington said. "That suitcase looks like
it will do just fine. Still, if the wardrobe people don't feel it
goes with your costume, you may be asked to switch. Would
you be comfortable with that?"

"That wouldn't be a problem," Annie said. "Someone
else could use this one."

Ms. Kensington smiled. "Thank you. That's very kind.

They'll keep it all straight and make sure it gets tagged with your name if they do need to swap you. It may look like chaos in there, but actually it's very organized chaos."

Annie walked into the overheated trailer and was immediately swept into the action. She stammered that she was to be on the ferry, and that she would be carrying her own suitcase unless it was deemed unsuitable for her costume.

"That will be just fine," the harried assistant said, as she snatched the little valise from her hands, brusquely thanking her. The assistant flipped the valise open. She thrust a clipboard into Annie's hand with a command: "Sign this!"

Annie looked over it as the razor-thin young woman tapped her foot, clearly wanting the clipboard back. Finally Annie scrawled her name in the two places required.

The assistant looked over the signatures suspiciously, then peeled off a label at the bottom of one page and slapped it on the inside of Annie's valise. A second label from the same sheet went on a large clear shopping bag. "This will be for your clothes," the assistant said. "Give the bag to the wardrobe women. Move along."

Annie was passed along to two other women who pulled clothes off long racks and piled them into Annie's arms. Annie felt a little dizzy from the heat in the room and the terse demands of each person.

The women pushed her toward a screen that served as the "dressing room" for the trailer. She dressed quickly, folding her own clothes into a neat pile. Finally she stepped out with her bundle of clothes in her arms. The women clucked at her for a moment, taking her clothes away from her and pulling her limbs this way and that as if she were a particularly stubborn mannequin. They pulled on the seams of her clothes and the hems until they were happy with the way each piece hung on Annie's slender frame.

"Here, dear," the oldest woman said as she thrust the bag into Annie's hands. "Put your clothes in here. I've already put another sticker on it with your name and number—I find those little labels that they give you from the forms fall off and they're almost impossible to read." She opened Annie's coat and pressed another sticker inside. "This is your number to pick up your clothes after the shoot. Micki will take the bag as you leave the trailer. Now, hurry on to far end there and Vernee will do something about your hair."

Annie raised her hand to her straight blonde hair. She hoped whatever Vernee was going to do about her hair wouldn't involve scissors.

Vernee turned out to be a tiny African-American woman with steel gray hair and a wide smile. "You have that deer-in-the-headlights look," she said, patting a swivel stool next to a tall, lighted mirror. "Don't worry—we haven't lost an extra yet."

Annie smiled. "It is all a bit overwhelming."

"Just part of movie magic." Vernee began twisting Annie's hair up almost before she could sit completely down on the stool. The woman's hands almost seemed to blur in the mirror as she stuck a nest of hairpins in to keep up the neat twist. Then she sprayed a cloud of something over the result. The entire process took less time than it had taken for Annie to skim-read the form and sign it.

"You're good," Vernee said. "You wouldn't believe how many people fidget, and I have to chase them all over the stool. Try not to touch your hair. This stuff will hold in a hurricane, but it's better not to handle it."

"I won't," Annie promised.

The woman smiled again, her eyes nearly vanishing into the fine wrinkles on her face. She patted Annie's hand. "You have a good time now."

Annie nodded mutely and stood. She shuffled toward the rear door of the long trailer and back into the bitter cold. A young woman wrapped in a long striped scarf snatched the bag from Annie and told her it would be at the trailer after the shoot. "Don't lose your number," the bundle of scarf warned.

"I won't," Annie assured her, and she actually felt relieved to walk through the cold to the collection of other dressed extras. Alice was already in the group. Annie looked over her friend's costume. She wore a dark, wool pencil skirt with a vaguely military-style suit coat over it. The style and cut of the coat made Alice's waist look tiny. Alice's red hair had been swept to one side to spill over her right shoulder. They'd added strong makeup that brought out Alice's eyes and made her lips look almost pouty.

"You look dazed," Alice said.

"I feel thoroughly processed," Annie admitted. "They certainly are efficient. But I also must say that you look very glamorous!"

"Yes, I've been trying to figure out how to run off with this outfit. It's not really a good match for the weather, but I love how skinny it makes me look," Alice said. "I'd like Jim to see me in this getup." Alice still wasn't completely over Jim Parker, the dashing photographer who had come into

Stony Point like a whirlwind. He had spent several delicious weeks in town, working on a book about lighthouse legends. Just as quickly, he had moved on.

"I don't know," Annie said. "Are you sure he doesn't have a heart condition?"

"I might be willing to risk it."

"I notice they didn't feel it necessary to dress me in something like that," Annie said looking down at her own more serviceable costume.

"All this dark color would overwhelm you," Alice said. "They're going for a sweeter look for you."

"Sweeter, meaning boring?"

Alice smiled. "I think you look lovely."

"Well, I'm glad they were quick," Annie said.

"I guess you have to be if you're going to get this many people ready and still have time to shoot the scene," Alice said. "I spent last night searching online to find out what being an extra is really like. Mostly, it sounds like a lot of standing around and waiting."

"At least we have heaters."

Slowly, more and more people joined the group. Between the huge heaters and the huddled body heat, it wasn't nearly as bitterly cold as Annie had expected. Her toes grew cold, but otherwise, she mostly just got tired of standing in the same place for so long.

She smiled when Vanessa and Mackenzie joined the crowd. Both girls were giggling, their cheeks pink with excitement. Since they were teenagers, they got by without having to wear dresses. Vanessa wore slim wool pants and a darling sailor-look coat. Mackenzie wore cuffed jeans, boots, and a tattered, oversized man's coat.

"You'll never believe this," Vanessa said to Annie and Alice. "One of the wardrobe ladies said Logan Lariby is going to be in this movie!" She punctuated the announcement with a squeal. "I'm so glad I didn't have to wear the scarecrow costume."

Mackenzie gave her a playful shove. "My beauty will shine through anyway. Logan will spot me across the crowded wharf. Our eyes will lock. He'll never even see you."

Vanessa made a scoffing sound, and then turned to Annie and Alice. "Even just seeing Logan Lariby would be fantastic. I hope he's in this scene."

Annie looked at Alice and raised her eyebrows. Alice just shrugged.

"I'm sorry," Annie finally said. "I don't know who he is."

"Only the hottest guy in the entire world," Mackenzie said. Her tone was dripping with "Duh!"

"Oh, OK," Alice said. "The hottest guy in the whole wide world." She grinned. "I thought that was Jim Parker."

Annie laughed as the two teen girls rolled their eyes. "I don't mean old guys," Mackenzie said.

"Hey," Alice said. "I'll tell Jim you said that, and he won't tell you two any more ghost stories."

Annie laughed. "That must be the world's most empty threat," she said. "Jim loves to tell ghost stories. I don't think you could get him to stop telling them with anything short of a gag."

Mackenzie flapped a hand at both of them. "I think we were talking about Logan Lariby."

"Logan is on *Breaking Hearts*," Vanessa added.

"I don't watch much television," Annie admitted, suddenly feeling rather old and out of it. The girls just shook their heads, and then they caught sight of someone else they knew and rushed over to share the news.

"I remember being like that over John Travolta," Alice said. "Can you imagine? All that hair!"

Annie laughed, thinking back to her own teenage crushes. Then they were practically plowed into by a breathless Peggy Carson. "I saw him!" she gasped.

"Logan Lariby?" Alice asked.

"No, of course not," Peggy said. "Matt Rusher. Wally loves his movies. We've seen all of them. Oh, I wish Wally were here."

Now Matt Rusher was a name Annie recognized. She and Wayne had gone to all his action movies for years. After Wayne died, Annie hadn't seen any of the actor's more recent work. "My husband liked his movies too," Annie said, and then a thought struck her, and she laughed. "I expect Ian will be excited too. He said he likes movies where things blow up."

"Rusher hasn't made any movies lately," Alice said. "I thought maybe he was sick or something."

"He didn't look sick to me," Peggy said, then smiled dreamily. "You know, some men just look more distinguished with age."

"Someone talking about me?"

The women turned to see Stony Point's mayor, looking dapper in a long trench coat and porkpie hat. "We weren't," Alice said. "But we could be. You definitely look very distinguished in that outfit."

"Matt Rusher is going to be in this movie," Peggy said, nearly jumping up and down. "He's going to be in this scene!"

"Really?" Ian's eyebrows went up. "The movie people didn't say anything about blowing stuff up in Stony Point. I heard this was going to be one of those warm family films for cable. That doesn't really sound like a Matt Rusher kind of movie."

"Maybe he's branching out," Alice said.

"I suppose," Ian said. He held up a suitcase and said to Annie, "It looks like you and I are both going on the ferry."

"Oh, that'll be fun," Annie said.

Just then a nervous young man rushed over to shout at the group that they needed to get into position for the scene. He called for the ferry riders to follow him and sent the "greeters" on to follow another shivering man with a clipboard. Annie was starting to think clipboards were the badge of movie making.

As the group was rushed onto the boat that would represent the ferry, Annie took a moment to be grateful that her wardrobe included gloves and a scarf. The wind blowing across the water was vicious. "We want you to stand near the rails as the ferry approaches the pier," the young man yelled. "Then when the ferry docks, someone will signal you. You simply walk off in an orderly way. We'd like you to smile and look toward the crowd on the pier."

The young man went through the crowd and paired up a few people. He tugged Annie closer to Ian. "You two be a couple," he said. "As you walk off, kinda look at each other and smile, please."

"No problem," Ian said cheerfully.

Finally the young man told them not to stare at or interact with any of the actors. Annie looked curiously as a young man walked up onto the boat carrying a canvas duffle. Unlike most of the people, he was wearing neither a hat nor a scarf. Even his coat was slightly open. Annie assumed it was to make him easy to recognize in the crowd, but she suspected he must have been cold.

He was a nice-looking young man. Annie doubted he could be much older than Vanessa. He had big brown eyes and a thick scruff of dark hair. That must be Logan Lariby, Annie thought. She smiled at the thought that teen idols still seemed to have a lot of hair these days. The young actor slipped through the crowd to take his mark. As he passed by Annie and Ian, he nodded politely, making eye contact with a smile.

After Logan was in place, everyone else was shown where to stand in relation to the actor. Ian and Annie stood next to the rail, and Annie fought to keep her teeth from chattering. Ian moved closer to her to block some of the wind. "Having fun yet?"

"Surprisingly, yes," Annie admitted. "It's fascinating, and until we moved to the boat I wasn't even terribly cold."

They chatted quietly for a few minutes, and then the boat started up and moved away from the pier only to make a tight loop and circle back. When they were finally pointed in the right direction, someone bellowed, "Action!"

Annie looked out toward the pier as she had been directed. The wind made her eyes water, but she kept a smile plastered on her face as the pier grew closer and closer. She was grateful for Ian's attempts to keep as much wind as possible away from her.

Finally the boat docked, and Annie saw the crowd on deck begin to move toward the gangplank. She slipped her arm through Ian's and smiled up at him as they walked. He looked down at her, his eyes warm. For a moment, it was fun to pretend to be walking with her beau.

From the corner of her eye, she saw Logan slip by them and hurry across the pier. That's when she saw that he was meeting Matt Rusher. The tall action hero had more gray in his hair than Annie remembered from his films, but he had the same ramrod-straight stature and icy blue eyes.

For an instant, Annie was sure the actor was looking directly at her, and he looked furious. Then she remembered that she wasn't supposed to be looking at the stars. She looked back up at Ian, giving him another laughing smile.

The actor is probably supposed to be angry with Logan, Annie thought. He probably wasn't looking at me at all. She shook her head slightly at her own silly notions. Clearly she didn't have a future in movie making if she was going to take every glance seriously.

Finally someone shouted, "Cut!"

Annie's first adventure in movie making was over.

—6—

nnie joined the group on the pier as they waited to hear if they would have to repeat the scene. She looked around and soon spotted Alice and Peggy huddled against the cold wind and looking longingly toward the huge heaters near the wardrobe trailers. Annie headed toward her friends with Ian following close behind.

"You two looked great coming off the dock," Peggy gushed as they approached. "Like the perfect couple."

"Must be that fine Butler family acting," Annie said with a grin.

"We Butlers are method actors," Ian said, placing his hand over his heart dramatically. "We have to feel it to show it."

Alice grinned and pointed off toward the edge of the crowd. "You two aren't the only cute couple. Look over there."

Annie turned, but all she saw was the crowd. Then two women blocking her view separated and stepped out of her way. Annie could see a narrow gap all the way down the wooden guardrail that ran along the side of the pier. She spotted Logan Lariby chatting with Vanessa and Mackenzie. Even from where Annie stood, she could see how Logan smiled whenever Vanessa spoke and leaned toward her to hear over the wind.

"I wonder what Kate will think about that," Alice said.

"I'm sure it's nothing serious. After all, the movie crew

won't be in Stony Point all that long," Annie said. She looked around through the crowd. "Where's Matt Rusher?"

"Oh, he didn't stay to talk to us common folk," Alice said, disapproval dripping from her voice. "The second they yelled 'cut,' he stomped off. As far as I know, he hasn't said a word to anyone. That young boy is definitely the nicer actor in this film."

"That's OK," Ian said, putting an arm around Alice. "I would rather not have Matt Rusher charming the ladies of Stony Point anyway. That's my job."

"And you do it well," Alice said. "Doesn't he, Annie?"

"He does." Annie looked around the crowd. "I wonder how many more times we'll film today. I imagine these things are normally filmed more than once."

"Oh, definitely," Alice answered. "From what I read online, we can expect to spend half the day here doing the same thing over and over."

"At least you look good doing it," Annie told her.

The wind flapped Annie's skirts as she waited for the call to get back on the boat, but instead the nervous young man with the clipboard passed through the crowd with a totally different message. "You may all go," he said. "The director said we're going to wrap for today. We'll need to shoot this scene again tomorrow. Stop at wardrobe and pick up your clothes. Please come tomorrow dressed as you are today; just bring something to change into after the shoot. You can leave any props you may have with the wardrobe people."

Annie caught the young man's arm as he passed. "This suitcase is mine," she said, holding up the small valise, "but I can leave it if you prefer."

"No need," the young man said. "You can take it home. Just bring it with you tomorrow." He paused. "Unless you think you might forget to bring it with you. Then you should leave it. We want to be certain to have continuity in all the scenes."

"I'm sure I can remember to bring it back," Annie assured him.

"Good. That'll be fine then."

Ian stepped into the man's path before he could hurry away. "Why don't we just finish filming the scene now? We still have hours of daylight. It's early, and the weather is unusually good. You can't really count on two good days in a row this time of year. You might get them, but you might get a blizzard."

The young man looked even more nervous. Then he leaned closer. "You're Mayor Butler?"

Ian nodded.

"The problem isn't the weather." He looked around. "It's Matt Rusher. He's having some kind of temper tantrum. I'm sure the director will have him calmed down by tomorrow. Do you really think the weather won't hold?"

Ian shrugged. "It's Maine. You never know."

"If it's not one storm, it's another," the young man said. Then he slipped away to pass the word around about the shoot in the morning.

"I must say, it's rather disappointing to think that Matt Rusher is a prima donna," the mayor said. "His movies have been some of my favorites. I consider *Let God Sort Them Out* to be a classic. And *Endless Blood* was good too."

"Sounds like art films for sure," Alice said.

"Maybe not art," Ian quipped, "but I know what I like."

"Well, I definitely think I don't like Matt Rusher," Alice said.

"Maybe there's something really bothering him," Annie said. "Oh well, it looks like we'll be doing this again tomorrow."

Ian smiled. "I can think of worse things than standing next to you on a boat for a few hours."

"In the freezing cold?" Annie asked. She shivered. "I'm heading home for some hot chocolate."

A cheery voice spoke from behind them. "You could go get some from The Cup & Saucer."

They turned to see Peggy coming up beside them. "I'm on my way there now," Peggy said. "And I've walked by several people saying they're going there too. So I need to be sure to beat them, or my boss will be in a terrible temper."

"Sounds like a plan to me," Alice said. "As long as I don't have to see anymore ill-tempered men today."

Annie shivered as the cold wind whipped around her skirt and coat. "I think I'll just go home."

"Wait!" Vanessa hurried toward them, hauling Logan Lariby along by the arm. He didn't look as if he minded a bit. "I want you guys to meet Logan."

She introduced the young actor, and he nodded and spoke politely to each of them.

"Logan plays Matt Rusher's son," Vanessa explained. "They don't get along."

"In the movie," Logan interjected. "We get along just fine in real life. I'm looking forward to learning a lot from Mr. Rusher. He's been in the movie business longer than

I've been alive. He started out in makeup effects, and he's done just about every job there is before becoming an actor and a star."

"He sounds impressive," Alice said.

The boy nodded and looked pleased to have defended his idol.

"I understand filming is stopped today because something upset Mr. Rusher?" Annie asked.

"Matt's really particular about everything being just right," Logan said. "I'm not sure what the problem was though." Then he grinned. "I don't mind getting off work a little early today. Vanessa's going to show me around Stony Point."

"That shouldn't take long," Alice said, laughing. "Not a lot of touristy things are open this time of year."

"That's too bad." Logan looked around. "It's beautiful here. I love all the snow. I was glad we were filming here now. The snow makes it feel a lot more like Christmas than twinkle lights on palm trees back in California."

"It must be hard being away from your family at Christmas," Annie said.

"It's just me and my dad," Logan said. "And he's not much into Christmas. So I'm not really missing anything. I've really enjoyed being here so far."

Vanessa's eyes grew large. "Why don't you come to our Christmas party?"

"Christmas party?" Logan echoed.

"Yeah, my mom and her boss and their club," Vanessa said. "They're having a big Christmas party. It'll be fun. I'll be there. We'll show you a nice New England Christmas."

She turned to look at Annie and Alice. "Don't you think that would be fantastic?"

"I don't know," Logan said, his face clouded. "I don't want to butt in. And I'm not totally sure how long we'll be here. We don't have a lot of scenes to shoot here, but whenever you do outdoor work, there's no telling how long it can take. Mr. Rusher told me that."

Annie reached out and patted the young actor's arm. "Well, we'd love to have you at the party if you're still in town. I don't think we've even set a date for it yet."

Logan smiled tentatively. "Thanks. I will if I can."

"Well, let's go start the Stony Point tour," Vanessa said. Logan nodded at the others politely before Vanessa towed him away.

"Poor boy," Alice said. "He doesn't know what hit him."

"Vanessa's a lovely girl," Ian said. "I suspect that's what hit him."

"I wonder what happened to Mackenzie," Annie said.

"Maybe we should check the water," Alice answered, laughing. "Vanessa might have given her a little shove to be alone with Logan."

They all laughed at that, and then Ian turned to Annie. "Can I talk you into joining me for hot chocolate now?"

"Sorry," Annie said. "Grey Gables is actually closer, and it comes with a warm cat for my lap. I'm heading home. I'll see everyone tomorrow."

"Do you want me to walk you to your car?" Ian asked.

Annie laughed and patted his arm. "No thank you. I remember where I put it."

"I'll walk with you, Annie," Peggy said. "I need to get

back to the diner pronto. I'll have to change in the break room. Let's go get our clothes."

The two women walked away quickly to the wardrobe trailer. The figure who was bundled up in a long scarf stood outside the trailer next to an open door. A short line formed at the door, but it seemed to move quickly. In only scant minutes, Annie was facing the lady in the bundle of coats and scarf that said, "Number please?"

"Number?" Annie echoed.

"Your pick-up number?" the bundle said. "For your clothes."

"Oh right!" Annie unbuttoned her coat and took a quick look at the sticker inside. She rattled off the number, and then buttoned her coat back up as quickly as possible before the wind could suck the remaining warmth from her body.

The bundle turned and shouted the number into the trailer. Soon a package of clothes sailed out the door, and the bundle caught it smoothly and handed the bag to Annie.

"Thank you," Annie said, stepping out of the way.

"You're welcome; see you tomorrow."

Annie nearly answered, "But I won't see you." Instead, she stood to one side and waited for Peggy to collect her bundle of clothes.

Peggy gave her a quick hug and said, "I've really got to run. The boss is going to have my head."

Annie called after her. "Be careful of the ice."

Peggy just waved a hand as she trotted away. Annie shook her head and walked carefully, especially after she hit the paved parking lot. Piles of charcoal gray snow, pushed aside by the plows created a kind of labyrinth to weave through on the way to the car. This far from the bustle of the film crew, the snow dampened the sounds. Even the wind seemed to have died down some.

Annie often found Maine winters like that. You could be in the middle of town and turn a corner, and suddenly you could feel completely alone and isolated. It had something to do with snow dampening sound, she supposed, and perhaps, the uniquely New England way the wind seemed to change direction with every gust. Annie shivered, thinking there was a kind of creepy Stephen King feel to the effect.

She spotted her burgundy Chevy Malibu and shifted the bag of clothes to the same arm that held the valise so she could rifle the pocket of her coat for her car keys. Suddenly, she felt a hard shove at her back. She stumbled to her knees, and someone wrenched the valise out of her hand.

"Hey!" Annie yelped.

Annie turned to see a man in a long dark peacoat and a watch cap pulled down low on his head running away across the parking lot with her valise in one black-gloved hand.

"Stop, thief!" she yelled after him.

7

Suddenly the thief must have hit a spot of black ice. His feet flew out from under him. He slammed into the pavement, jarring his grip loose on the valise. It skated along the ice, disappearing under a hulking SUV.

Annie heard shouts behind her and turned to see Alice and Ian hurrying toward her. The thief must have heard them too, because he scrambled to his feet and ran off. Alice stopped beside Annie to help her up, while Ian chased after the thief.

"Are you all right?" Alice asked as soon as Annie was standing.

"I think so," Annie said, her voice shaky. She looked down at the heavy silk stockings she wore and saw they were torn and dotted with blood from her scraped knees. "Wardrobe is not going to like me."

"They'll get over it," Alice said. "Did the thief get your purse?"

"I wasn't carrying one. He grabbed that old valise. I guess he thought it was a purse?" Even as she said the words, they seemed unlikely. The little hard-sided suitcase didn't look anything like a purse.

"He must have thought there was something valuable about it," Alice said. "Hopefully Ian will catch him and get it back."

"Actually, the thief dropped it when he fell," Annie said.

"It slid under that SUV."

Alice walked over to the SUV and bent low to look under it. Then she walked around to the front of the vehicle and came back with the valise. "It slid all the way out the other side. That must have been a heck of a fall the guy took. I bet he feels it tomorrow."

Just then Annie caught sight of Ian slipping between the cars toward them. "I'm afraid the thief got away," Ian said. "Are you OK?"

"Nothing but some skinned knees," Annie answered. "I'll be fine. But I think I'll take you two up on the invitation to have some hot chocolate at The Cup & Saucer. I don't think I'm ready to be alone right now."

"Good idea," Ian said. "Why don't you ride with me. I can send someone to collect your car."

Annie waved that off. "No, really. I'm good to drive." She took the valise from Alice and unlocked her car door. "I'll meet you both at The Cup & Saucer."

"You should bring the valise in," Alice said. "We ought to look it over again. Maybe the thief was after that valise in particular. Could be another mystery in the works. After all, it did come out of your attic."

Annie shivered. "I certainly hope not."

At the diner, Peggy raised her eyebrows at Annie's skinned knees. Annie was really glad she'd had some wipes in the glove box of her car. She'd wiped off most of the blood and cleaned the bits of gravel from the scrapes. The alcohol in the wipes had stung, but Annie figured that was better than getting an infection. Still, the wipes couldn't do much to make her stockings look like anything but tattered rags.

It was obvious Annie had been in some kind of a mishap.

"It looks like you didn't follow your own advice about being careful in the snow," Peggy said.

"I tried," Annie told her.

She was grateful when Peggy didn't give in to her usual curiosity and pepper Annie with any other questions. Instead, the pretty brunette quickly found the group a table well away from the front windows and near a heat register. "Warmest spot in the diner," she said. "Well, outside the kitchen, that is."

"Thanks," Annie said. "I can use some warming up."

"I'll bring some hot cocoa right away," Peggy said, looking around the group. "Unless you want something else?"

"Hot chocolate will be fine," Ian said. Alice nodded as well.

While they waited, Annie set the valise on the table. They opened the case and looked it over closely. It was a well-made piece, but they couldn't find anything special about it. There was no false bottom, no lumps or tears in the smooth cream-color lining where something could be hidden. They went over every inch of the leather covering and found no bulges or mysterious clues scribbled into the leather. They looked over every bit of stitching, and it all looked original. The lock didn't have any secret message slips crammed into the keyholes.

"It's just an old battered valise," Annie said. "The most mysterious thing about it is that both locks are broken. I can't imagine why anyone would think it had value."

"The thief probably thought you had something valuable inside it," Ian said.

Just then, Peggy arrived with their cocoa and a plate of

warm muffins. "They just came out of the oven," she said. "I thought you might like some."

"You're the perfect waitress," Ian told her. "You know what we need even before we do."

Peggy beamed at him, then leaned over to whisper to Annie. "How did you skin your knees?"

"I fell down in the parking lot near my car," Annie said, smiling at the thought that Peggy had kept her curiosity in check for nearly five whole minutes.

"After someone mugged her," Alice added.

Annie gave her friend a sharp look. She hadn't really wanted everyone in Stony Point to know about the incident. "It was nothing," Annie said. "He must have thought this old suitcase was valuable. But he wasn't a terribly skilled mugger. He ended up falling down on the ice and losing his prize."

"Well, good," Peggy said fiercely. "Too bad he didn't knock out some teeth too."

"I'd imagine film crews might draw all sorts of disreputable types," Ian said. "I'll speak to someone about this. And I'll alert Chief Edwards as well."

Annie put her hand on the mayor's arm. "I wish you wouldn't. I'd like to simply forget about this. I'm sure this is an isolated incident."

Ian frowned, but nodded. "If you want. Though I do plan to speak to Chief Edwards." He raised a hand as Annie opened her mouth to protest. "I won't mention any names, but he needs to know there was an incident. I would like them to keep an eye on the filming. I don't want anything like this happening again."

Annie nodded at that. She stretched her legs and winced at the tight ache in her knees. "You know, I think I'm going to go on home," she said. "But first, I plan to drop this valise off with the prop master. He's probably back at his room at Maplehurst Inn by now. He can look after it. I still feel sure this is some kind of fluke, but I'll feel safer if he looks after it."

"I'll go with you over to the inn," Alice said. "Safety in numbers!"

"Thanks," Annie said. "I will feel better when I'm not carrying that around." She gestured at the valise. "I'm sure it's just a case of a slow-witted thief, but I find I'm not as fond of that suitcase now. If it's going to turn out to be a mystery, I'll cheerfully hand it off to someone else."

"I'll call you later," Ian said. "Just to see how you're feeling."

"That's not necessary," Annie said. "I'm fine, but it is sweet of you." She patted Ian's arm again and then followed Alice out of the diner, trying not to limp on her stiff knees. So far, being a movie extra had been a total pain. Maybe a tough first day would mean a really easy second—at least she hoped so. Her aching knees reminded her that she wasn't a kid anymore, following Alice from one crazy adventure to the next and always coming away with some kind of scrape.

Though she suspected she was going to be achy in the morning, Annie's knees felt less stiff by the time they'd walked the short blocks to Maplehurst Inn. The tall colonial-style building seemed to blend into winter with its buff-color siding and stone facade. Only the forest green trim caught the eye.

Annie was glad to slip inside and out of the cold. She

saw that a cozy fire burned in the fireplace of the large lobby. Several people she recognized from the morning's movie shoot sat in chairs around the fire. She looked carefully, but none of them were the young prop master.

Alice walked to the front desk and asked if Linda Hunter, the owner of the inn, was around.

The girl behind the counter nodded, looking concerned. "Is there a problem?"

"No," Alice assured her. "Linda is a friend of ours."

The girl smiled, more relaxed. "She's talking with the chef, I believe." She leaned closer and dropped her voice. "We've had our hands full. We don't normally have so much business this far into winter, and they're working on menus out of our normal winter food stocks."

While Alice chatted with the young woman, Annie walked closer to the group around the fire. "Do any of you know which room the prop master is in?" she said. "I want to leave this valise with him."

An older woman looked Annie up and down, and Annie immediately recognized the thin face from the wardrobe trailer. "Are those ours?" the woman asked, pointing a slightly heavy knuckled finger toward Annie's stockings.

"Sorry, yes, they are," she said. "I fell in the parking lot next to the pier."

The woman nodded. "Don't worry. We have more. They aren't real silk."

The other gray-haired wardrobe lady—this one with a kind round face—leaned forward. "Are you all right, dear?" she asked. "Betty here doesn't mean to overlook your injury. We just always think about clothes first—occupational hazard."

The thin-faced woman blinked. "Oh, you were injured?"

Annie looked down at the scrapes on her legs. "A little. It's nothing to worry about," she said. "I'm glad you have more stockings."

Betty stood and took a step closer to Annie, bending slightly to look at her knees. She shook her head. "We'll have to put something over those scrapes before filming in the morning," Betty said abruptly. "They might show through the stockings. Can you cover those up, Pat?"

The round-faced woman rolled her eyes and said, "Yes, we'll just paint them with liquid bandage. It shouldn't be a problem. I'm glad you weren't hurt badly. It's icy out there. You should be careful. Several of our people have fallen down."

"Mostly the young folks," Betty interjected. "They're always in such a hurry. Slow and steady is the way to stay safe."

Annie smiled a little at that, thinking of the amazing bustle inside the wardrobe trailer, and the way she felt rushed through. These wardrobe ladies certainly weren't slow when it came to work.

"I guess we're not exactly used to ice," Pat said. "We're all going to look like the walking wounded by the time we leave at this rate. I even saw Matt Rusher limping earlier; not that he'd ever admit to anything as clumsy as falling down."

Betty turned a wicked grin toward her friend. "Maybe that casting director gave him a kick in the shins. I saw him making a pass at her yesterday."

"Oh you!" Pat said, shaking her head. "You're such an old gossip."

Betty sniffed. "I'm not that old."

"I would imagine the poor man fell. I certainly know

how easy it is to fall out there," Annie said, hoping to head off an argument. "Mostly, I'm looking for the prop master. I want to leave this valise with him."

"Ah, Samuel is another of our walking wounded," Pat said, nodding her head.

"Did he fall down?" Betty asked.

"Must have. He was nursing his elbow when I saw him earlier." Then she peered closer at the bag. "Is that one of ours?"

"No, it's mine," Annie said. "But I'm carrying it in the scene, and I'd rather leave it with him."

"Well, you're in luck then," Pat said, nodding off toward the door of the dining area. "That's him right there. Oh dear, looks like he hit more than his elbow."

Annie turned and immediately recognized the young man in ratty jeans. She saw he had a scrape down the side of his face. For a fleeting moment, she wondered if he could have gotten the scrape after knocking her down and grabbing the valise. But the young man was far less bulky than the man who had mugged her.

Annie gave herself a little shake for being so silly. She knew the props department needed more suitcases, but the young man would hardly knock her down to get one!

She walked across the room to him. "Excuse me, aren't you the prop master for the film?"

The young man looked at her curiously. "That's right," he said. "I'm Samuel Ely."

"I'm Annie Dawson," Annie said. "I was one of the extras from this morning. I had this valise that I carry in the ferry scene. The suitcase belongs to me, but since I'll be carrying it in tomorrow's filming, I was wondering if I could leave it with you tonight?"

"Sure," Samuel said with a shrug. "I can put it in my room. But it's fine for you to just bring it with you tomorrow."

"I would rather not," she said. She took a deep breath and added. "Someone tried to steal it from me in the parking lot. I'm sure it was just a coincidence since the suitcase is empty, but I think I would feel better if I didn't take it home."

"Someone tried to steal it?" The young man took the case and looked it over for a moment. "It's a nice little case and in decent shape, but it's not valuable. I have several cases up in my room worth more than this one. I can't imagine why someone would want to steal it."

"I can't either," Annie said, "but I know I'll feel better if you have it."

"No problem, just remind me of your name again? I have a great memory for stuff, but a horrible memory for names. I'll need to put your name on the case so they get it back to you for the shoot tomorrow," he said.

"Annie Dawson." She felt a rush a relief. She hadn't realized how tense the whole incident had made her. "I really appreciate it."

"Happy to help," he said. "I'll just run up and dump it in my room." He reached out for the bag, then winced and rubbed his elbow. "The ice around here is deadly," he grumbled, and then managed a smile for Annie. "Maybe I'll see you at the shoot tomorrow. Good night, Mrs. Dawson."

"Good night," she said.

She walked back over to Alice with more of the usual spring in her step. She was relieved to have passed along one mystery. Alice was leaning on the front desk talking with an attractive woman Annie recognized as Linda Hunter.

"Nice to see you, Annie," Linda said. "Alice was telling me you've had a rough morning."

"It actually was a nice morning except for one incident," Annie said, with a sideways glance at Alice. "I'm feeling much better now."

As Annie spoke she noticed Linda glance past her toward the front door with a stressed look.

"What's the matter?" Alice whispered, she began to turn toward the door, but Linda grabbed her arm.

"Don't look," Linda said. "Our most antagonistic guest just came in, and if you turn around he's going to think we're talking about him."

Alice laughed lightly. "Which we totally are."

Linda gave her a warning look, and then pasted a warm smile on her face. "Good afternoon, Mr. Rusher," she said. "May I help you?"

"I simply wanted to compliment you on your lovely inn," the actor said smoothly as he stepped up to the desk. Annie noticed he favored one leg slightly, just as the wardrobe women had said. Then he turned and smiled at Annie and Alice. "Don't I know you lovely ladies from somewhere? You were at the shoot this morning, right?"

"That's right," Alice said. "I'm surprised you noticed."

"I never miss seeing a beautiful woman," he said. "And I've always had a weakness for redheads."

Alice smiled. "You didn't seem to be quite so enraptured by my hair this morning when you pushed me out of the way as you stormed across the pier."

"Oh, I'm sorry about that," he said. "I hope you'll

forgive me. I was out of sorts this morning. Movie making demands so many small parts work together, or it's just a train wreck. This film marks a new chapter in my career, and I want to be sure everything works."

"It is unusual for you to do a movie where nothing blows up," Alice said.

Rusher laughed at that, but Annie wasn't sure he really was amused. "I'm getting a bit long in the tooth for jumping off trains and punching out villains," he said. "I want to exercise my more subtle dramatic skills now."

Annie snuck a glance at Linda and saw the innkeeper's mouth was practically hanging open. Clearly she was seeing a different side of the actor than she'd seen before too. Annie couldn't help but wonder what had brought out this unexpected pleasantness.

"It's too bad we couldn't finish the shoot this morning," Annie said quietly. "We'll have to go back out in the cold tomorrow."

"Sometimes delays can't be avoided," he said, turning his warm smile on her. "I believe you were on the ferry this morning, weren't you? That was probably especially cold."

"It was a bit chilly," Annie said, "but not as bad as I'd expected. And being part of a movie is interesting."

"Just don't feel too bad if your role ends up on the editing floor," the actor said. "You wouldn't believe how many of my best lines have never seen the light of day. There has been a couple that I believe would have ended up being as iconic as 'Go ahead, make my day,' or 'Yippee-ki-yay …'"

"Yes," Annie interjected, remembering the rest of that "iconic" line and not really wanting to hear it in the lobby of Maplehurst Inn. "I imagine that would be frustrating."

She still wondered why the actor was being so attentive to them. Then she realized she might not be thinking fairly about the man. She hadn't actually seen what caused him to become angry, and Logan had seemed quite impressed by the man. Maybe he'd been having a bad day earlier and was trying to make up for it now. Or maybe he was a stranger in a strange town, and he just wanted a bit of company.

Matt Rusher turned his eyes and his charm back toward Alice. "I hope you ladies don't have to drive too far to get to the set," he said. "This weather can be dangerous."

"We're used to the weather," Alice said. "In Maine, you have to be ready for anything."

The actor nodded, letting a brief awkward pause gather. "Well, it was nice to meet you ladies. I don't believe I caught your name."

"Alice MacFarlane," Alice said.

"Pleasure to meet you." He took her hand and held it a moment in a glove-clad grip. Then he turned to Annie and looked at her quizzically. Annie felt an irrational urge to refuse to tell him her name, and the silence lingered a moment too long to be comfortable.

"Annie Dawson," Alice said. "She can be shy."

"Shyness is a rare trait in a beautiful woman," the actor said, bowing over her hand until Annie had an alarming image of the man kissing her hand. Thankfully he stood back up without any kissing, and Annie slipped her hand quickly away.

"Well, I'm sure I will see you ladies tomorrow," he said.

"See you then," Alice said.

The tall, broad-shouldered actor turned and headed for the winding staircase that led to the guest rooms. "Wow," Linda said quietly as soon as he was out of sight. "That was certainly different. I wonder if he has some kind of split personality. That's the first time I've seen him open his mouth without complaining."

"Oh," Alice said, her eyes sparkling. "A mysterious stranger acting oddly. Do you suppose that's a clue?"

"A clue to what?" Linda asked. "Your ability to charm actors? You must have done a better job than me. He's been a horrible pain every time I've spoken to him."

"Must be Annie," Alice said. "She brings out the lamb in the lions."

"I don't know," Linda said, grinning at her friend. "As I remember, it was your hair he commented on first."

Annie stared thoughtfully up the staircase and felt a stir of unease. Something told her the actor hadn't really been particularly attracted to either of them. She thought something completely different was happening and wondered if Alice's teasing remark might be on target. Could Matt Rusher's behavior be some kind of clue?

— 8 —

Annie gave herself a mental shake for being so fanciful. Getting mugged was making her see a mystery behind every smile. It was definitely time to get in a bit of quiet time crocheting in front of a roaring fire with a cat in her lap.

"I think I'll head home now. I've had more than enough excitement and adventure for one day," Annie said. "I'll see you tomorrow on the set, Alice. It was nice to see you again, Linda."

"Nice to see you," Linda said.

"Do you want me to walk back to your car with you?" Alice asked. "I know your knees must be sore."

"No, I'm fine."

"Then, I think I'll hang around with Linda for a while in case any other handsome actors want to fall for me."

"I can't promise you any handsome actors, but I did want to talk to you about some baked goods," Linda said. "And I'm willing to beg. I've brought back in as much of my staff as I could, but a lot of people are traveling this time of year, and we flatly cannot keep up with the appetites of these movie people."

"If you feed them Alice's baked goods, you might never get rid of them," Annie warned as she turned away with a smile. She'd told Alice that she would do an amazing business if she sold her delicious muffins and coffee cakes. Now

Linda's desperation to feed so many hungry movie people might just give Alice that chance to show off her skills.

Annie walked out of the inn, still smiling. She felt much safer now that the valise was out of her hands, which was probably just as silly as fretting over the motives of an aging movie actor. Maybe he just liked being admired. She knew Hollywood was pretty focused on youth culture. That was probably scary for a man like Matt Rusher who'd made a living being big and tough, and now was definitely showing his age.

The drive home was uneventful and Boots greeted her with her usual pushy affection. Annie spent the rest of the evening at home just as she'd planned with a warm cat in her lap and soft yarn in her hands. By bedtime, she was convinced the attempted valise snatching was totally random, and she fell asleep almost looking forward to the next day's shooting.

That happy feeling came to an abrupt end when her alarm clock beeped her awake in the dark of early morning again. Annie crawled out of bed, moaning at her aching knees. The skin on them seemed to have shrunk in the night, and they hurt every time she moved her legs.

"Who thought being an extra was a good idea?" she mumbled as she limped to the bathroom to hold cold cloths to her knees until they felt less like her bones might burst through at any moment. Then she went back to get dressed, trying to walk as normally as possible.

As she laid her clothes out on the bed, Boots gave her a supportive head bump, and Annie scratched the soft fur behind the cat's ears. "Sorry to leave you alone again today," she said. "We'll fit in some more lap time when I get home."

Since she was going to have to change into stockings in the wardrobe trailer anyway, Annie slipped into a pair of close-fitting knit pants under her skirt and pulled on boots. She carried her costume shoes in the bag with the rest of her change of clothes.

Just as she was finishing up, she heard a knock at the door. Annie cut her eyes toward the clock. Who would be visiting while it was still dark? She hurried downstairs and crept across the front room to peer through one of the long windows. Alice stood on the porch, grinning toward her.

Annie threw open the door. "Did we have a plan to meet?"

"No," Alice admitted. "But I thought you might still be jumpy from yesterday and wanted to suggest we drive in together. Besides I've been up for hours. I baked so many muffins and coffee cakes that I reek of cinnamon. I've already delivered them to Linda so I warn you, my car smells like Christmas. Sniff." She held out her arm, and Annie leaned close to catch the smell of warm spices.

"Wow, you smell delicious! So you took Linda up on her request for baked goods?"

Alice nodded. "Baked and delivered. And being up so early definitely showed me that I do not want to be a professional baker. At least Divine Décor and Princessa Jewelry parties are always held at respectable hours." She leaned closer to look Annie over. "I half expected you to have dark circles under your eyes from being awake all night worrying. But you look terrific."

"I'm not worried anymore," Annie said. "I don't know why I let my imagination run away from me like that yesterday.

But I'll take you up on the ride, just for the heavenly scent alone. But I suggest you stay away from Matt Rusher. I half expected him to kiss my hand yesterday. If he catches a whiff of you, he's liable to lick your hand like a puppy."

"Now there's an interesting image to start the day," Alice said. "He does look good, but he comes across kind of slick. I've been there and done that."

Annie nodded. Now that she thought about it, Matt Rusher did remind her of John MacFarlane. They were both strikingly handsome and polished. And being an actor, Matt was surely capable of being every bit as skilled a liar as John. "It's a wonder John never became an actor," Annie said.

Alice snorted. "Too much work."

Annie grabbed the shoes and the rest of her change of clothes from the couch where she'd left them and followed Alice out the door. The early morning was still dark but not nearly as cold as the morning before.

"We're having some kind of warm front," Alice said. "And I'll take it as long as it doesn't come with freezing rain."

They settled into Alice's convertible and headed toward the waterfront. Annie couldn't help but notice that Alice's Mustang didn't feel as snug and warm as her Malibu. She shivered slightly.

"Yeah," Alice said, seeing the shiver. "The convertible doesn't button up as tight as I'd like this time of year. But every time I get cold, I just think of how much fun the car is in the summer."

Annie laughed. She had to admit, she couldn't imagine Alice driving anything else. They pulled into the parking lot soon after that, and Annie shook her head as she looked toward all the lights and trailers. "Still looks like the circus has come to town."

"I think it has," Alice agreed.

They hopped out and headed directly to wardrobe, feeling like old pros at the extra's job.

Both of the wardrobe ladies looked down at Annie's pants as she walked in. "An interesting addition to the costume," Betty said dryly.

"I didn't quite think you'd OK it," Annie teased. She slipped the pants off from under the skirt. Annie's pink scraped knees stood out sharply against her fair skin.

"That's right," Betty said, frowning. "You tore your stockings."

"We have more," Pat chimed in, sorting through a small multi-drawer chest and handing Annie a pair. "At least nothing on the dress or coat looks torn or stained. Perch here, and I'll paint your knees with liquid bandage. It has a pale tint and should cover the scrapes nicely. We'll have to give you a minute to dry before you slip into stockings. I hope they aren't too painful."

"They were a little stiff when I got up, but the more I walk, the better they feel," Annie said as she sat on the edge of the chest Pat had pointed toward. The round-faced wardrobe lady painted the liquid bandage over Annie's scrapes. It stung a bit, but Annie held very still.

"Good girl," Pat said, patting her arm like a fond aunt. "I always like working with extras. They don't whine so much."

"Some of the actors though, whew," Betty moaned. "You would think we were throwing them outside naked."

"Not that we wouldn't," Pat chimed in. "We do whatever the script calls for."

Annie smiled at the banter between the ladies. It was obvious they had been working together for a long time. "I imagine you both must have some amazing stories from this work."

"A few," Betty said.

"And a few we'll never tell," Pat added. "Now, you're all set. Just be careful as you put on the new stockings."

"I'll need my valise too," Annie said as she walked behind the screen to change quickly.

"A valise?" Pat's voice carried from the front. "I don't see you on the prop list."

"It's the one I was carrying yesterday when I saw you at the inn," Annie called out. "Do you remember? It's leather in shades of brown. I gave it to Samuel Ely to put with the other cases." Annie stepped out from behind the screen with her knit pants neatly folded and her boots in her hand.

"Well, maybe he hasn't brought it yet," Pat responded. She gestured toward the small pile of luggage. "Do you see it?"

Annie peered at the pile. At first, she didn't. Then she saw a familiar-looking corner and pointed. "I think that's it in the back."

"Of course," Betty grumbled. "It would have to be in the back." The thin woman pushed her way through the pile of luggage and retrieved the small valise. "This it?"

Annie gave it a quick look. "Yes, that's it. Sorry to make you go scrambling."

"Sammy didn't tag it either," Betty said. "I'm going to

have to give that boy a talking to."

"Well, I did dump it on him suddenly," Annie said, feeling badly for creating any discord. "It's my fault."

"Don't worry," Pat said, patting her arm. "Betty's growl is worse than her bite. Go and get your hair done, dear." She peered down at Annie's knees. "The liquid bandage seems to be working perfectly. I think your knees will look fine on camera. In a distance shot, no one will see the scrapes. If the camera were going to linger, then we'd have to send you to makeup. Vernee has magical ways to make even the worse flaws vanish."

"I'm sure the cameraman won't be interested in my knees," Annie said.

"You never know." Betty and Pat laughed as Annie moved on to get her hair swept back up in a quick twist. All too soon, she was finished in the trailer and back out in the chill of the pier. Still, she could tell the wind was not as biting as it had been. She spotted Alice chatting with Ian and walked to them. "Good morning," she said.

"Good morning," Ian answered. "I hope you're feeling better."

"Yes," Annie said. "I think I'm back to normal. Is it wishful thinking, or does the wind seem warmer this morning?"

"No, we're definitely in for a warm snap," Ian said. "We're going to see some snow melt. I know my roof will appreciate that. I don't know how the film crew will feel about it though. They came looking for a snowy Christmas town."

Alice laughed. "Just tell them to give us a little while. If you don't like the weather, wait an hour, and it'll change."

"I'd hate to see it all melt," Annie admitted. "I really do

want a white Christmas, even if I don't get to spend it with LeeAnn and the twins."

Annie looked at the other extras standing in small groups, and then she spotted Vanessa standing near the pier railing with Logan Lariby. "Did you chat with Vanessa?" she asked Alice.

"We spotted them right away," Alice said. "That young man looks smitten to me."

"Yes, I think that's a genuine case of smittenness," Ian said. "I'm not surprised. She is a very pretty girl."

"And just as lovely inside as out," Annie added. "I wonder if Kate knows about her new friend."

"I don't think Vanessa could have kept it a secret if she wanted to," Alice said. "She was playing tour guide after the shoot, remember? I expect Kate knew before we got our first sip of hot cocoa yesterday."

Annie nodded. The Stony Point gossip network was extremely efficient. "I wonder how Kate feels about it."

"How would you?"

"Worried," Annie said. "As I remember, that's how I felt about everything when LeeAnn was that age."

"And yet," Ian interjected, "LeeAnn grew up to have a happy home and family. I expect Vanessa will be just fine as well."

Annie nodded. "I'm sure she will."

"But I'm glad it's not my worry," Alice added.

Annie had to agree. The young actor certainly seemed very nice. She wondered if Kate had met him. Maybe she could ask her. That made Annie jump. "Oh, I forgot," she said. "I need to stop at A Stitch in Time after the shoot and get some more crochet thread for a project I'm making. I ran out during my crochet marathon yesterday. Do you mind?"

"No, I expect I'm going to be seeking out some more hot cocoa in town anyway," Alice said.

Just then the young man who had moved the groups of extras around the day before walked through and sent everyone to their places. Annie noticed that Logan kept talking to Vanessa in the group of extras on the pier until the young assistant virtually dragged him to the ferry.

As Annie stepped up on the gangplank to the ferry, she felt a creeping unease, as if someone was watching her. She turned around and scanned the crowd. Matt Rusher was standing at the edge of the crowd of extras, staring at her. The charming man of yesterday was gone, and he had the same fierce glare that he'd turned her way when she'd first seen him. What could the man possibly have against her, she wondered.

Then he saw her looking back; his face lightened, and he smiled and nodded. Annie smiled slightly and nodded back. Then she slipped her hand through Ian's arm, stepping closer to him for comfort.

Ian looked down on her in surprise. "Cold?"

"A little," Annie said. "Plus, I'm practicing my character."

Ian patted her gloved hand on his arm. "Practice away," he said.

They made their way to the spot where they had stood the day before. The young assistant made slight adjustments in everyone's position based on notes on his ever-present clipboard, and then the ferry pulled out from the pier again, and Annie waited for the action to begin.

Though the small scene seemed to go smoothly, the director had them repeat it another five times. Annie's feet began to ache in the unfamiliar shoes, but thankfully she never really got much colder. The temperature was definitely rising. She wondered if her smile was starting to look a little strained. It certainly felt that way, although every time she looked into Ian's handsome face, his smile down at her seemed genuine and warm. "You Butlers are fine actors," she said.

"How's that?" he asked.

"You don't look the least bit tired of all this."

"Tired of spending time with the best-looking woman in Stony Point?" he asked. "I can't imagine."

"Charmer," Annie scolded lightly, but Ian's words gave her a slight ego boost, and her own smile felt less forced.

Still, the morning stretched on until Annie's stomach growled, and she knew it must be getting close to lunchtime. They finally must have had a shoot the director liked because they called it a wrap.

"The director wants to do interiors over the weekend, so we won't be shooting our last large group scene until Monday morning in the town square," the young assistant said as he wove through the crowd of extras. "If we need you, you'll get a call sometime over the weekend. Since it's a large group scene, it's likely we'll need everyone."

"Well, the town square should be warmer," Ian said as he rubbed his hands together. "I'm ready for some cocoa. Are you with me?"

"Not me," Alice said as she walked up to join them. "I'm having chowder—a big bowl of it. I'm starving."

"Oh, chowder sounds wonderful!" Annie agreed as they headed for wardrobe. She changed quickly and headed for the door of the wardrobe trailer.

"Aren't you forgetting something?" Betty asked dryly.

Annie looked around. "I don't think so."

"You need to leave the suitcase, dear," Pat said.

Annie looked down at the small valise and considered leaving it behind. After all, it had gotten her mugged. At the same time, she loved the warm colors of it and really wanted to use it in the coffee-table project. "This suitcase is mine," she said. "I brought it for the shoot."

"Oh, all right then," Pat said. "You have a nice day now."

Annie thanked the ladies warmly and said she'd probably see them Monday. Then she hurried out to join Alice and Ian. Alice held up the canvas-covered suitcase she'd brought but hadn't needed for the shoot. "I remembered to collect this in wardrobe," she said. "Are we set to go?"

"I am so ready," Annie said. "I can almost taste the chowder now."

"I'll meet you ladies there," Ian told them.

Annie and Alice headed to the convertible and tossed the cases into the backseat before heading off. As they drove, Annie saw signs of melt everywhere. The pine trees were almost bare of the white trim they'd been wearing for days and a trickle ran down the side of the road where the plowed piles of snow were shrinking.

"If we get a lot of melt today, I hope it doesn't turn too cold tonight," Alice said. "The roads will get nasty if it does."

Annie nodded, though she didn't plan to leave Grey Gables for the next couple of days. That is, not unless she was struck by a sudden flash of inspiration about Herb's present. She sighed.

"Why so glum, chum?" Alice asked.

"Oh, I was just thinking about my son-in-law's Christmas present," Annie said. "I still haven't found anything for him that really jumps out at me."

Alice glanced sideways at her. "With how slow the mail moves this time of year, you probably should figure something out soon, or it's going to be a great after-Christmas present."

"I know," Annie said weakly. "Ian suggested a book. I know Herb likes to read, but picking a specific book is so hard. I don't know what he's read."

"You could get him a gift card to the bookstore there," Alice said. "Do they have one close by?"

"There's a little independent one in Brookfield," Annie said. "I heard the big chain store closed."

Alice nodded as she drove. "I guess it's a hard time to be a bookseller with those electronic book readers."

Annie shuddered. "I can't think of a less cozy way to read a book. It would just be something to pile on top of the laptop I rarely use. LeeAnn teases me about being a bit technophobic."

"She's not?"

"Oh, no," Annie said. "She and Herb love their computers. And you should see their cellphones. They do so many things—I'd never figure one out. The last time I was in Texas, I was telling them about a shop I had seen in Storm Harbor, and by the time I was done describing it, LeeAnn had found a photo of it. Her phone can search the Web. How crazy is that?"

"Maybe Herb would like some new electronic gadget," Alice said.

"Maybe." Annie made a mental note to ask LeeAnn about it, and then she smiled as they pulled onto Main Street. She was really ready for a hot bowl of chowder.

~9~

nnie followed Alice out of The Cup & Saucer, smiling with the cozy warmth that only a belly full of clam chowder brought her. She almost didn't mind the cutting wind—much. The sidewalk was completely clear now with the warm sun having melted off the small piles of snow that huddled in the shadowy cracks between each building.

Then she stopped and groaned in annoyance.

"What's the matter?" Alice asked.

"I promised the twins I would try to be green for the whole month of December. They're all gung ho about recycling at their school," Annie said. "I've always been careful about putting out the recycling, even in the snow. And last year I changed all my lightbulbs to compact florescent, even though sometimes they seem to take forever to give off any light. But I forgot to bring my cloth bag for the yarn I have to pick up at A Stitch in Time. I'll have to use one of Mary Beth's bags, and that's definitely a green taboo."

"I don't have a shopping bag either," Alice said, frowning slightly as she thought. Then she laughed. "Hey, how about the valise? You could put all the yarn you possibly want in it."

"Good idea," Annie replied, sighing with relief. The women stopped at Alice's car, and Annie grabbed her valise. She was so glad Alice had thought about that. She was sure the twins would quiz her on her green activities when next they called, and she didn't want to disappoint them.

She carried the case into the needlework shop. Kate smiled at them from behind the counter, while Vanessa leaned against it. Mary Beth was nowhere to be seen, but Annie knew that Kate and Mary Beth often worked every other day in the winter when the customer load was so much lighter.

"Ah, more movies stars," Kate said. "Did you two have as much fun during the filming as Vanessa?"

"I doubt it," Alice said, her blue eyes sparkling. "I didn't have any handsome young men swooning over me."

Vanessa rolled her eyes. "Logan wasn't swooning."

"He looked pretty swoony to me," Alice said. "Didn't it look that way to you, Annie?"

Annie held up a hand. "I'm not getting involved in teasing. I get enough of it myself. I did think Logan seems like a very nice young man."

"He is that," Kate agreed. "You would hardly know he works in Hollywood. I always imagined the young people in movies to be spoiled and out of control. He wasn't like that at all. He even helped haul some boxes off the upper shelves in the back room here. I thought Mary Beth was going to adopt him on the spot."

"That definitely doesn't fit the mold of the Hollywood wild child," Alice said.

"Logan would never be like that," Vanessa said loyally. "He doesn't even drink."

"He's not old enough to drink, is he?" Annie asked.

"Not legally," Vanessa said. "But he told me a lot of kids

he's worked with are already drinking or worse. He said that he had promised his grandmother not to do those things when he went into acting, and he's kept his promise."

"He sounds like a keeper," Alice said.

"I don't think we need to be considering keeping him," Kate interrupted. "I don't mind Vanessa spending a little time with him, but let's keep in mind that he won't be staying in Stony Point. And," she turned her attention solely to Vanessa, "you're both only in high school. You can talk about keepers after you graduate from college."

"That's not how you and Dad did it," Vanessa teased.

"And if that's not proof," Kate said, frowning slightly. "I don't know what is. Don't do what I did."

"I know," Vanessa said, holding up her hands in surrender. "Logan and I are just friends, really. Logan's great to talk to, and we have fun together. That's all. Speaking of which, I'm thinking I'd like to stay in town this weekend and not go with Gram and Pops to Vermont. Would that be OK?"

"You've had this trip planned for months," Kate said. "How do you think they'd feel about being thrown over for a boy?"

"Gram would be cool," Vanessa insisted. But then her face fell. "Pops wouldn't. I guess I'm stuck." She turned around and moped against the counter. Then her eyes fell onto Annie's valise. "Hey, cool suitcase."

"Thanks," Annie said. "I used it for the movie, and now I'm going to use it for carrying home some yarn. I'm embracing the green movement and not using plastic bags. Well, not today anyway."

"Some of our customers bring cloth shopping bags in

here," Kate said. "But a valise will be a first."

"I forgot my cloth bag," Annie said. "I guess I'm still new to being environmentally responsible."

"Her grandkids are making her do it," Alice chimed in.

Laughing, Annie admitted that they were.

Vanessa leaned closer to look at the small suitcase. "That is really a cool bag. I love the color, and it's so retro. Do you think I could borrow it for this weekend trip? It would be a perfect overnight bag."

Annie looked down at the valise. "I guess that would be fine. The locks are broken, but it closes fine. You weren't going to use it for checked baggage on a plane anyway, right?"

"No, I'm using it for crammed baggage in my grandparents' car," Vanessa said taking the valise and giving it a hug. "Thanks a ton. I really like it. It's all yummy chocolate and caramel."

Annie smiled. "That's what I liked about it too. I guess we sweet-tooth travelers have to stick together." Then she looked at her empty hands. "Now I don't have a bag for my yarn."

Alice laughed. "No problem, I'll go get the other suitcase." She pointed at Vanessa. "No falling in love with this one too."

"I promise," Vanessa said. "Mom, can I go put this in the car and then walk down to Maplehurst Inn? I promised to meet Logan there for a hot cocoa next to the fire."

"That's fine," Kate said. "Tell Logan I said hi."

"I'll walk out with you," Alice said. "I'll be right back with the other case."

As soon as the two had left the shop, Kate pulled out

her cellphone. "Just a sec," she said to Annie. Annie smiled as Kate called Linda Hunter and asked her to keep an eye on Vanessa when she got to the inn. "Vanessa has pretty good sense, but that young actor is awfully good looking," Kate said into the phone. "I just don't want her getting any ideas about going upstairs to his room."

Linda must have promised to keep an eye on them because Kate smiled and thanked her before slipping the phone back into her blazer pocket and turning to help Annie. Annie picked up more of the fine crochet thread she was using for her filet crochet runner, and then looked over a new display of baby-weight yarn that had metallic strands twisted in.

"I love this," Annie said. "You know, I think I have the perfect pattern for this. You talked me into it last summer. The lace sweater vest?"

"The one with the nice long points at the front hem?" Kate said. "I love that one. I think you're right, this yarn would be great for it. Are you going to make one for yourself or someone else?"

"Myself," Annie said. "I've made all my presents." Then she felt the nudge of guilt about Herb's gift, but mashed it down. Whatever she gave her son-in-law, he definitely wouldn't want a lace sweater vest.

"You should get the blue," Kate said, pulling Annie out of the small guilt attack. "It would be perfect with your coloring." Kate helped her pick out enough skeins in the same dye lot to do the vest.

When Alice came back, Annie piled the yarn into the small suitcase. The women chatted for a while, and

Alice picked out some more silk ribbon for her practice embroidery projects.

"I've already embroidered silk flowers on a pair of bedroom slippers I bought for my mother, a vintage handbag I bought for my sister, and a whole set of place mats," Alice said as she counted the things off on her fingers. "By the time Stella is ready, I'm going to be fluent in these roses. They aren't hard, really, but we know how picky Stella is."

Finally they headed back out into the cold. Annie was looking forward to getting home. Alice had to drop a Divine Décor order off to a client at the southern end of Main Street. Then she continued south a bit and made a wide circle back around to catch Grand Avenue past the waterfront.

"Aren't we going the long way?" Annie asked.

"A little," Alice admitted, "but I hate turning around and coming back the same way I went. Sometimes you see interesting things when you take the scenic route."

"That's fine," Annie said, although she could have done without the scenic route. Her knees were beginning to ache again, and the glamour had worn off the movie business somewhere about the fifth time they took the same short boat ride in a frigid wind. Still, she couldn't help but look for the wardrobe trailers as they passed. It was hard to believe how quiet the area seemed now.

The Mustang reached a long empty stretch of road near the waterfront, and they heard the roar of an engine behind them. A dark SUV rushed up on their bumper. "Hey, no passing here," Alice grumbled, glaring into her rearview mirror.

The SUV driver clearly didn't care as the vehicle crossed

the double yellow line and moved up beside Alice's convertible. They rode side by side for a few moments. Alice let up on the gas to slow her car so the other car could get by her. Instead the SUV slacked off on speed also and kept pace beside her.

"Well, pass already!" Alice yelled, waving at the SUV to move forward. "This isn't a one-way road, buddy. If someone comes around one of the curves coming up, there's going to be an accident."

Annie put out a hand to brace herself against the dash. Something about the SUV's dark windows as it kept pace with them seemed ominous. There was no glimpse of the driver inside the vehicle.

The SUV suddenly swerved over, as if trying to get in their lane right on top of them. Alice leaned on the horn as the two vehicles bumped hard. The little convertible was rocked by the impact, but Alice kept it on the road.

"This guy's crazy," she yelled. She was gripping the steering wheel so hard, her knuckles turned white from the effort. "What is his problem?"

The SUV still didn't pass, and again it came over on them, bumping Alice's Mustang and shoving them toward the narrow shoulder and the rocks just beyond that.

"It's trying to force us off the road!" Annie exclaimed. She reached into her coat pocket and fished out her cellphone. With shaking hands, she dialed 911 and told the operator what was happening. Her voice sounded high, almost shrill in her ears. She fumbled and nearly dropped the phone when the SUV made contact with the convertible again.

The Mustang ran along the shoulder for a moment,

kicking up slush, before Alice could wrestle it back into the road, barely in time for the turn ahead. Side by side, the two vehicles turned onto Ocean Drive, the road that ran in front of Annie and Alice's homes. Alice spotted a pickup coming their way in the other lane. She hit the gas hard and jumped ahead so the SUV couldn't bump her again. The SUV driver must have spotted the truck barreling toward it, because the driver wrenched the big vehicle to the right and dropped behind Alice's convertible.

That's when the women heard the sound of a siren. The SUV turned off onto the gravel road that led to Butler Lighthouse. The driver used the road to make a turnaround, racing off down Ocean Drive in the opposite direction. Alice pulled off the road into the circular drive for the carriage house, and both women waited for the police car as their hearts pounded.

The police car pulled into the drive behind Alice's convertible. When the officer got out, so did Annie and Alice. The officer walked up to the convertible, shaking his head as he looked at the damage to the beautiful car.

"We got a call someone was trying to run you off the road," the officer said. He pointed at the dents. "It looks like he made a good effort. It's awfully early in the day for a drunk driver."

"That driver wasn't drunk!" Alice said, and Annie saw tears in her friend's normally bright blue eyes. Alice loved that convertible, and Annie knew it must hurt to see the side so banged up. "He might have been crazy, but he seemed in control of his vehicle. He turned around when we heard your siren," she said. "He must have run right past you. He was driving a big dark SUV."

The officer nodded. "I did pass an SUV. I didn't know it was involved in the incident though. You keep saying 'he'; did you get a good look at the driver?"

Both women shook their heads. "The windows were dark," Alice said.

"Did either of you get the license number?"

Annie and Alice both looked at each other. Neither had. "Wow, some mystery solvers we make," Alice said with a shaky laugh.

"That's perfectly understandable," the officer said gently. He pulled off his leather gloves and pulled his cellphone out of his pocket. "The experience must have been pretty scary. Why don't you ladies go in out of the cold? I'm going to take some photos of the damage, and then I'll come in and take your statements."

They nodded and headed up the steps into Alice's house. Even as stressed as she was, Annie couldn't help noticing all the charming touches Alice had added to the place for Christmas. Her friend certainly was a skilled decorator, and her house was a testament to how lovely the Divine Décor items worked with the older-style homes in Stony Point.

"Do you want some tea?" Alice asked. "I would offer coffee, but I definitely don't need to be hyped up any more than I already am."

"Do you think this had anything to do with my mugging yesterday?" Annie asked, hugging herself as a wave of shivering passed over her. Alice's house was warm and snug, but Annie wasn't sure she was going to feel warm for a while.

"I don't know," Alice said softly as she turned to walk

toward her cozy kitchen. In a quieter voice, she added. "I'm wondering if it might have something to do with John."

"Your ex?" Annie said, stopping short in surprise.

"I know it's probably silly, but we didn't part on the best of terms last time," Alice said with a sigh. "Or any time actually."

Annie remembered John MacFarlane's last trip to Stony Point. The man had frightened her, but even though she didn't have a very high opinion of him, she couldn't quite imagine him deciding to run them off the highway for no clear reason. Now if money were involved, then she could see it. "Has he contacted you looking for money?" she asked.

"He hasn't contacted me looking for anything," Alice said as they reached the kitchen and she began to fill the kettle. "And I would love to keep it that way."

Soon the police officer came in and took their report as they sat around her small table sipping hot tea. They had few details, but Alice mentioned her ex and their rocky relationship.

"Do you have reason to believe he is in the area?" the officer asked.

"No," Alice admitted.

"Has he threatened you?"

"No."

"We'll definitely look into him as a possibility, but it doesn't sound like the most likely option," the officer said as he dutifully scrawled John's name in his notebook.

Then Annie told him about the mugging in the parking lot at the pier. The officer listened intently as she described it, taking careful notes. "I tend to think that event is not re-lated to this either," the officer said. "We do sometimes get purse snatchers and pick pockets in that area, though not so much this time of year. Still, the movie set could draw all kinds of people."

Annie nodded. "I just wanted to be sure to mention it, especially since I saw an SUV in that parking lot."

The officer smiled slightly. "I'd imagine you'd find SUVs in lots all over Stony Point," he said. "They're fairly popular around here."

Annie nodded, struck suddenly with a silly thought. Joanna and John would strongly disapprove of anyone driving such a non-green vehicle. As she fought back a giggle, she realized how close to hysteria she really was. What was going on?

~ 10 ~

The police officer thanked them and said they'd get a call whenever the police knew anything. "You be sure to call if anything else happens," the young man said.

As soon as he left, Annie invited Alice to spend the night with her. "I'm feeling a little shaky," Annie said, "and you look like you are too."

"I think that's a great idea," Alice said. "Let me collect some things and button up the house for the night. Then I'll come right over."

"All right, I'll go on then."

Annie grabbed the small suitcase full of yarn from the car and cut across between Alice's house and hers. Anywhere the sun had fallen on the lawn, the snow was slushy, and Annie was glad she'd worn her snow boots.

Boots met her at the door, meowing in complaint. "I know, I've been gone a lot lately," Annie said. "I'll be home all day tomorrow." She scooped up the gray cat and hugged her. "And I have a surprise for you. One of your favorite people is spending the night." Boots purred in reply as Annie stroked her fur.

She carried Boots into the kitchen and put the kettle on for more tea—she wasn't sure she'd had enough comfort beverage. Then she dumped some cat food into the small ceramic bowl on the floor. Boots dove into the bowl as if Annie had been starving her as well as neglecting her social needs.

"Poor kitty," Annie cooed. Then she jumped when she heard a rough pounding on the front door. "Goodness, what's that?"

Annie hurried to the door. She was startled to find Alice in the doorway, pale and shivering as she clutched a tattered package in her hands. "Alice!" Annie gasped as she hurried her friend inside. "What's wrong?"

"I wanted to collect my mail before I came over. I found this in my mailbox," Alice said, handing the package to Annie.

It was a small padded envelope, stained and ripped in several places. The return address was torn completely away from the rest of the package. A sticker on the front of the envelope said it had been accidentally damaged in handling.

"Looks like it lost a battle with the post office," Annie said.

"Look inside."

Since the end was torn out of the envelope, it was easy to see the jewel case inside. It was clear plastic with a crack across the face. Inside was a CD with no label. Someone had scrawled, "I'm coming for you," across the face of the CD.

"What's on the CD?" Annie asked.

"Creepy music," Alice said, her voice still shaky. "I only listened for a few seconds. I didn't want to hear anymore while I was all by myself. Do you have a CD player?"

Annie nodded and led Alice into the living room. She picked up a small CD player from the floor next to her chair and ejected the CD of Christmas music she'd been playing while she worked on Christmas projects. Alice placed the new CD inside and started it. The music was all instrumental with a low almost mournful wail. Annie felt a chill just listening to it. "I agree; it's creepy," she said. "Do you have any idea who sent it?"

Alice shook her head. "I wondered if maybe it was the same person who drove the SUV," she said. "What if the guy has been stalking me for a while, and he's only just now done enough to get noticed?"

Annie looked at her friend's frightened face. "Then I think we should call the police back," she said.

"And tell them what? I got a Halloween CD in the mail, and I don't know who sent it?" Alice asked. "That officer took us seriously before because we had the evidence of a battered car, but you know how quickly they'll mark you down as a neurotic woman living alone. Maybe I'm making too much out of this."

Annie considered arguing with her friend, but thought of all the times she'd hesitated to call the police herself. She knew how easy it was to second-guess yourself.

"Besides," Alice said. "What would they do about it? The package is so beat up, it doesn't even have a return address."

Annie nodded. "All right. But if anything else weird happens, we have to report this too."

"Fair enough," Alice said. "Look, I feel OK now. I'm going to go back and get my jammies." Alice laughed, but her voice still sounded strained. "It'll be good to just settle down and relax. I'm making myself crazy."

"Well, here, put on my coat anyway," Annie said. "You'll give yourself pneumonia wandering around in just a sweater."

Alice slipped into the coat and hurried out carrying the package with her. Annie watched her from the side windows, not wanting to take her eyes of Alice until she knew her friend was safe.

"A mugging, a crazy driver, and a creepy package," Annie murmured. *What do these things have in common?* she asked herself. *Which ones are related?*

What mystery had they gotten themselves into this time?

When Alice came back, the two women agreed not to talk about anything creepy. "I think we've had enough mystery in the last two days," Annie said. "If we're going to sleep tonight, we need a different topic."

"OK," Alice said. "How about men? I noticed you and Ian looked pretty cozy on the ferry during the shooting."

"We were told to act like a couple," Annie said. "It was acting."

"Well, I must say, you and the mayor are excellent actors," Alice teased. "All those meaningful gazes and sparkling eyes."

"Oh, you couldn't possibly see our eyes from the pier."

"We could," Alice insisted. "Just ask Peggy. The sparkle was dazzling."

Annie laughed, glad her friend was feeling more her normal self again. Still, she was eager to get off the subject of Ian. "So, when are you going to see Jim again?"

Alice sighed. "I have no idea. He finished his lighthouse project and started something new. He's doing a book on abandoned places."

Annie raised her eyebrows. "Like?"

"Ghost towns, abandoned prisons, and hospitals," Alice said. "Even abandoned buildings right in the middle of cities, if the interiors are interesting enough. It's amazing what people will just walk away from. He told me he was going to start with places in the United States, but the publisher is hinting at a second book that will show places all over the world."

"Sounds fascinating and kind of creepy."

"Jim is very excited about it, but unfortunately a lot of these places are way out in the middle of nowhere," Alice said. "No cellphone reception, no email, and no post office some of the time. Jim doesn't seem to mind. He's as happy roughing it as he is staying at a nice hotel. But I don't hear from him much lately."

"And you miss him."

Alice smiled ruefully. "I was getting used to having him call me a couple times a week. Honestly, Annie, you could talk to Jim for the rest of your life and never manage a dull conversation. He's been so many places and seen so many things."

Though Annie knew Jim was a great storyteller, she still thought Alice sounded very much like a woman in love. She wondered if Alice even knew how badly she was falling for Jim. "He probably misses you too," she said.

"He better." Then Alice laughed, and the shadow seemed to lift. "Enough about Jim, or you're going to have to spill about Ian."

"What's to say?" Annie asked. "You know Ian and I are just good friends. Anything else is just a figment of your imagination."

"Right," Alice said. "If I didn't know better, I'd think you were me back in my John MacFarlane days."

Annie looked at her quizzically.

"Back when I was Cleopatra, the queen of denial."

Annie shook her head. "No denial. All right, I admit it. I know Ian would like for us to be more than friends. He's pretty clear about it. But you know how it is ..."

"For you, there was only Wayne Dawson."

Annie's eyes shone for a moment, and she nodded.

"I can't say I know what it's like to lose someone like that," Alice said. "But if you do ever find you're ready to move on, I won't be surprised if our fine mayor is waiting."

"Are we done with love lives now?" Annie asked. "I know I'm thoroughly uncomfortable."

Alice laughed again. "Always my goal. We could talk about Vanessa's love life for a while."

"As much as I think Logan is very nice, I would love a totally different topic."

"But if men and mystery are off limits, what do we talk about?" asked Alice.

Annie picked up the Christmas CD from the table and idly turned it in the light so it sparkled like an ornament. "We could talk about Christmas. I noticed your house was gorgeous. I thought you said you'd only done a little bit, but it looked like you'd gone all out to me."

Alice shrugged. "I love Christmas," she said. "I don't intend to let it slip by just because I'm alone. I love the sparkle and the colors and getting presents." Then she grinned. "Still, if you think that was 'all out,' you should see it when I'm really inspired. One year I bought a tree so big I had to cut the trunk to about this short at the bottom." She held up her fingers with a few-inch gap between them. "It hid all my presents. Not good. Looking at my presents is one of my favorite things."

"Your presents?" Annie laughed. "Here I was thinking I would hear all about the spirit of giving."

"I love it when people are in the spirit of giving me things," Alice said, grinning. "I admit it. I never grew up. I'd make a list for Santa if I thought the old guy would come through for me."

Annie shook her finger at her friend. "You can't fool me. I happen to know there isn't a greedy bone in your body."

"You say that even though you have seen the convertible I bought myself," Alice said with the laugh. Then her face fell as she remembered the damage her beloved Mustang had taken.

Annie patted her arm. "I'm sure a body shop can make it look just like new again."

Alice nodded. "I'll have to go get estimates in the morning and call the insurance company. But for tonight, how about a movie?" She held up a red paper envelope. "A movie came in the mail today too. It's a comedy, just what we need."

"Great," Annie said. "I'll make the popcorn."

The rest of the evening passed in a pleasant blur of giggling and crunching. By bedtime, they both finally felt they'd put the day behind them. The next morning, Alice insisted she needed to get an early start on the whole insurance thing. "You know," she said, "maybe this was all some weird road-rage attack. Maybe the guy just hated convertibles. I'm ready to just get my car fixed and focus on Christmas."

"Good attitude," Annie said. Still, she watched as Alice walked back to her house. And stood watching for several more minutes, in case Alice came back with some new scary discovery. When nothing happened, Annie finally relaxed and started planning her own day.

She looked over at her project bag and wondered if she should settle down with some crocheting. She also considered bringing some Christmas things down from the attic. Maybe she should be like Alice and decorate for herself.

Finally she settled on an idea. She would pull out her laptop and go online to see if she could get an idea for the perfect book for Herb's Christmas present. She carried the computer out to the kitchen table and stared out the window pensively while she waited for it to boot up. This had certainly been a strange couple of days.

When the computer was ready, she opened her Web browser and clicked on the link to her favorite online bookstore. As she clicked through page after page of books, she put several on her wish list to look back over later for herself, but nothing specific jumped out at her for Herb. "I wish I could just give him the bookstore," she said. Maybe Alice was right and a gift card to the bookstore was best.

Annie remembered how much her grandmother had disliked the idea of handing out gift cards. "You might as well just admit you haven't paid attention to what people like," Betsy had said once when Annie's grandfather had suggested giving everyone gift cards to save time and shipping costs.

Annie sighed. "There has to be some answer. Some way I could give Herb the bookstore without something so impersonal as a gift card."

She aimlessly clicked through some links until her eyes hit something that just seemed to leap out at her. Electronic books! Herb loved gadgets and books! Quickly Annie began a search for electronic book readers and read the specifics for each one. Finally she picked a nice lightweight reader that came with a certificate for two free e-books. She bought a lovely leather case to go with it. She could have them gift-wrapped and shipped directly to Texas.

Annie sat back with a warm sense of accomplishment. She was willing to bet Herb wouldn't shrug off this present! And the next time she was in Texas, maybe she'd even try it out. She might like one of her own.

Then she looked down at the computer that spent most of its time cluttering up her dresser and shook her head. "I might as well admit it," she told Boots. "I'm an old-fashioned girl."

As she shut down her computer, the warm glow of accomplishment faded a bit as her mind turned back to the last two days. Annie pushed the computer to one side and grabbed a slip of notepaper and a pen. She decided to be methodical about the frightening events that had happened to her—and now Alice too—while she was still feeling the warm glow of solving the mystery of what to get Herb for Christmas.

She made a list of the strange events. Someone had tried to steal the valise. Someone had tried to run them off the road. Someone had sent Alice a strange spooky CD. Were these events related?

Looking at the list, it looked as if more things were tied to Alice than to Annie. "So probably the valise doesn't really matter," Annie said. Then she nearly shot upright. She had loaned the valise to Vanessa before the weird package or the near calamity on the highway. What if someone went after Vanessa?

Annie pulled the cellphone out of her sweater pocket and dialed A Stitch in Time. Mary Beth answered the phone with her usual bouncy greeting.

"Hi Mary Beth. This is Annie," Annie said. "Is Kate there?"

"Hi Annie. Sure she is. One second."

Annie tapped her toe nervously while she waited for Kate to come to the phone. She would feel terrible if the valise caused any trouble for Vanessa. Finally she heard Kate's warm, slightly husky voice. "Hi Annie."

"Hi Kate," Annie said. "I was just wondering if Vanessa got away on her trip?"

"She sure did," Kate said with a laugh. "And she's already texted me three times to see if Logan Larriby happened to come by the shop and ask about her. I am certain she would have kept that up all day, but Robert told her that there was a law against texting in a moving vehicle."

"I'm pretty sure that's just for the driver," Annie said.

"Vanessa tried to tell him that, but apparently he was adamant." Kate laughed. "It could be he was trying to help her stop thinking about that actor. She's going to drive her grandparents crazy by the time they get back."

Annie felt a surge of relief. "I'm sure they remember what it's like to be young and hyper-excited about things."

"I'm not sure I can picture Robert Stevens ever being hyper," Kate said, and Annie could hear the fondness in her tone. "That man is like a Zen garden in fishing gear. I wish Harry had taken after him a bit more."

Annie didn't quite know what to say to that, so she asked if Kate and Mary Beth had any more ideas about the possible Christmas party at A Stitch in Time. "We've had a few ideas, but we figured we'd save them for next week's meeting," Kate said. "Why? Did you have any thoughts?"

"Not really," Annie said. "The last couple of days have been so busy."

"Well, don't go getting starstruck on us with all that movie stuff," Kate said. "One girl with stars in her eyes is enough around here."

"I know I won't be running away to be a star anytime soon," Annie said. "Movie making seemed mostly cold—very cold."

They exchanged a few more light remarks before Annie hung up feeling much better. She got up and walked out to the front room and began taking the yarn out of the small canvas-covered valise and putting it into her project bag. The fine, soft yarn came in the most lovely, soft sherbet colors.

The sudden ringtone from her phone made her jump. She fished it back out of her pocket and checked the small screen. It was Alice. Smiling, Annie put the phone to her ear, expecting to hear her friend's bright voice.

Instead, the voice on the phone was definitely masculine and gravel-rough as it whispered into the phone. "I have your red-haired friend," the voice rasped. "If you want to see her pretty head without a hole in it, you'll bring me the valise."

~ 11 ~

Annie's throat closed in horror, and for a moment, she couldn't speak. Finally she managed to swallow and choke something out in a thin, high voice. "The valise?" The hand holding the phone shook, making the edge of the phone tap her ear. "But it's just an empty suitcase. What could you possibly want it for?"

"Don't concern yourself with why I want it!" the voice snarled. "Just give it to me."

"OK—of course," Annie whispered. "Just don't hurt Alice, please."

"She'll be fine as long as you do what I say. I want you to bring the valise to me tonight at midnight. I'll call back at eleven to give you exact directions so you can't set up any little traps. Be ready to leave when I call. If you follow my directions exactly, you'll get your pretty friend back in the same condition I found her. If not, you won't like the condition she's in when you see her again."

"Please, I'll do whatever you want."

"No cops. And don't think I won't know if you call them. It would be a shame if your friend spent Christmas in the hospital or the morgue."

The man on the other end of the phone coughed then, as if the hoarse whisper was hard to maintain. Finally he said, "I'll call back around eleven. Don't wander too far from your phone until then." With that, the call dropped.

Annie stared at the phone in her hands as she fought back a bubble of nauseous fear. She wasn't sure what to do. The man made it clear he'd be watching for any sign of the police, but Annie didn't want to face this by herself. She looked at the phone in her trembling hand, and then she took a deep breath and dialed Ian Butler.

Ian answered on the third ring and his voice sounded pleased. "Annie! To what do I owe the pleasure of this call?"

"Ian?" Annie said, embarrassed at the tremble in her voice. "Something terrible has happened."

"Annie, what's wrong? Should I come over? Where are you?"

"I'm at Grey Gables," Annie said. "A man just called. He said he's kidnapped Alice."

"What?" Ian's voice jumped to a low roar. "Why would a kidnapper call you?"

"He wants the valise I carried in the movie," Annie said. "It must be the same man who tried to steal it from me. And I guess it's the same one who tried to force us off the road."

"Forced you off the road? When did this happen?" Ian said.

"Last night," Annie said. "We didn't know it was related. Then Alice went this morning to get some estimates to fix her car. I didn't hear from her after that, but I got a call from her phone—only it wasn't her. It was a man with a horrible, raspy voice, and he said he wants the valise."

"Just stay calm," Ian said. "I'll come over, and I'm bringing Chief Edwards."

"No!" Annie yelped. "The man said not to call the police. He might be watching the house. I don't want him to see any policemen. He might hurt Alice."

"OK. Look, I'm going to tell Chief Edwards, but I'll tell him that he has to stay away from your house," Ian said. "Then I'm coming over. Tell me exactly what the kidnapper said so I can relay it to the chief. Did he demand you do something right away?"

"No," Annie said. "Not until midnight. But Ian, there's a problem."

"What problem?"

"That man wants the valise I carried in the film, and I don't have it," she said. "I loaned it to Vanessa to take on an overnight trip to Vermont with her grandparents."

"I don't remember the valise all that closely. Is it an unusual-looking piece?"

"Not really," Annie said. "The prop master had one just like it."

"That's the answer then," Ian said. "We'll get the one from the prop master. I'll pick it up and bring it to your house. Now, go over exactly what the man said so I can make that call to the chief."

Annie closed her eyes and concentrated on exactly what the horrible man had said on the phone. She described the raspy whisper and repeated the man's words as close to verbatim as possible."

"He sounds awfully melodramatic," Ian said. "Almost like a script from a bad movie."

"I know," Annie whispered, "and I feel like I've tumbled into a horror movie."

"Try not to worry," Ian said. "We're going to take care of this. I'll be there as fast as I possibly can."

"Thank you, Ian," Annie said softly. "I appreciate your help."

"It's going to be all right, Annie," Ian said. "I'm sure of it. Hold tight. I'll be there soon."

"OK," Annie said.

Annie put the phone down with shaking hands. She wasn't sure what to do with herself. She hoped Ian would be able to get the other valise. Then her eyes fell on the canvas-covered bag Alice had carried in the movie. It was about the same size, though it was the wrong color. The valise the kidnapper wanted was covered in leather. Still, at midnight, it might look close enough. Or maybe there would be another one in the attic. Somehow, she would have something to give the kidnapper. She had to.

Then she stopped and gave herself a little shake. There was no point in borrowing trouble. Samuel Ely had the second valise, and Ian was going to get it. She wouldn't need to find anything else. She had to calm down. She tried to concentrate on letting the nervous energy go, but finally just gave in and jumped up from the sofa.

She paced back and forth in the front room. Boots walked into the room and hopped up onto the small sofa, curling into the spot left warm from Annie's body. The cat watched her pace for a moment, and then meowed at her. Annie stopped and scooped the cat up in her arms.

"Oh, Boots!" she said. "I'm scared." She held the cat close and closed her eyes, saying a quiet prayer for protection for Alice.

She has just opened her eyes when she jumped at

the wet sound of tires biting slushy gravel in her drive-way. She wondered if it could be Ian, and she hurried to the long windows beside the door. "That was quick," she murmured.

An unfamiliar gray car rolled to a stop. Annie took a step back from the window so she wouldn't show from outside. The driver's side door swung open, and a man heaved himself to his feet. Annie took one look at the tousled silver hair and broad shoulders, and recognized the man instantly.

She put Boots quickly on the floor, and then threw open the front door. "Jim Parker!" she exclaimed. "What are you doing here?"

Jim walked toward her with the slightly swinging gait from his leg prostheses as he leaned on his long cane with each step. "Didn't Alice tell you I was coming?"

At the mention of Alice's name, Annie's stomach clenched again. How could she tell him about Alice? "She didn't know," Annie managed to stammer.

Jim stopped. "I sent a letter, a package really. Must be the crazy holiday mail. No wonder she wasn't home when I stopped. Do you know when she'll be back?"

"Jim," Annie said, softly. "You better come inside where we can talk."

Jim's blue eyes darkened like a storm. "What do we need to talk about?"

"Alice," Annie said. "Please, come in."

Jim followed her in, but as soon as he crossed the threshold, he said, "All right, I'm in. Where's Alice?"

Annie led him over to the sofa, in case he needed to sit

suddenly. Then she looked into his eyes. "Alice has been kidnapped."

"What?" Jim's deep rough voice boomed.

"Someone took her from her car, I think. At least, that's what I'm guessing since I think it's the same man who tried to force us off the road yesterday." Annie knew she was jumbling the story badly. "The man wants something ... a small valise I found in the attic."

"So, this is another of your mysteries?" Jim said, frowning slightly. "What's in the suitcase?"

Annie shook her head. "Nothing, Jim. Not one single thing. It's empty and even the locks are broken. Alice and I looked it over carefully when someone first tried to steal it. There is nothing hidden in the lining. It's just an old, cheap suitcase, but the kidnapper wants it."

"And you're going to give it to him?" Jim asked.

"I don't exactly have it," Annie said. "I loaned it to Kate's daughter for an overnight bag. But we already know there is nothing unusual about it, so I'm borrowing a valise that looks just like it. We're going to give the kidnapper that."

"We?" Jim echoed.

"I called Ian," she said. "Right after the kidnapper called me. He's contacting the police, but he'll tell them to stay away from the house. The kidnapper shouldn't know they're involved."

Jim began to pace, his cane thumping on the hardwood floor with each step.

"I don't like it," he said. "Why would someone grab Alice for something with no worth?" He stopped and looked at Annie intensely. "If they hurt her, I'll find them. I don't care about the police. I'll find them." His normally sparkling eyes had turned as gray as a nor'easter.

Annie swallowed nervously. She hadn't realized the charming, easy-going man could be so fierce. "We'll get her back, Jim." Then Annie was blinking away tears. "I'm so sorry that I got Alice involved in another stupid mystery. When this craziness started, we had no idea it was connected to that little suitcase. First the mugging, then someone trying to force us off the road. Then the strange message in the mail. We couldn't see how they were related until now. And now Alice is in danger, and it's all my fault."

"Alice would never want you to keep her out of any adventure," Jim said, stopping to pat Annie's arm awkwardly. Then he smiled a little and shook his head. "I know Alice well enough to know that you don't want to try to keep her out of trouble. My Alice is fearless. Don't blame yourself. The only one to blame is whoever took her. Now, tell me everything you know about this."

Annie nodded and began to pour out the whole story of the film, the suitcase, and every detail of what they'd experienced in the past few days. When she began to describe the frightening message scrawled on the creepy CD, Jim burst into laughter. Annie stared at him, baffled.

"Sorry," he said, pulling a handkerchief out of his pocket to wipe his eyes. "It's just funny about the package. I didn't mean it to be scary. I sent that with some photos from the last shoot. In the letter I explained that the songs were a 'ghost hunting' mix some guy gave me in Tucson. I thought she would think it was funny."

Annie smiled. "I'm sure she would have if the package had gotten here intact."

Jim nodded, and his face grew solemn again. "Well, I'll explain it to her as soon as we get her back. And we will get her back."

~ 12 ~

Annie turned when she heard the bite of tires on gravel again. This time it was Ian. He jumped from his car and hurried up the steps to Grey Gables. Annie had the door open by the time he reached it.

"Where's the valise?" she asked.

"I called Maplehurst Inn," Ian said. "The prop master didn't answer his room phone. I think we should drive over there. Then if we can't find him, we'll have Linda open the door for us, and you can pick out the right case."

"And just take it?" Annie said.

"This is an emergency, I'll pay for a replacement if it comes to that." As Ian spoke, the soft thump of Jim's cane on the wood floor drew his attention, and he looked around Annie. "Jim Parker? I didn't know you were here."

"I just got here," Jim said. "Landed right in the middle of it. Annie's brought me up to speed. We should go get the valise."

Ian smiled. "I'm not sure we need to made a group effort of it."

Jim nodded. "That's fine. You stay here then. Annie and I will go get the case."

Ian took a deep breath, and Annie could tell the two men were going to end up butting heads again. Something about Jim seemed to bring out the bullheaded streak in the normally easy-going mayor. "Look, we don't have time to fight," she said. "Let's all go get the valise."

"If that's what you want," Ian said. He looked toward the photographer. "Is it all right for us to take my car? It's the easiest to get out of the drive."

"Good plan," Jim said, smiling charmingly as he thumped past both of them and walked out to the porch.

"You should be careful about letting strange men in your house," Ian muttered to Annie as he helped her into her coat. Annie chose just to ignore him for the sake of keeping the peace. She couldn't imagine why Ian acted jealous of Jim considering it was clear Jim only had eyes for Alice.

Annie insisted that Jim ride in the front seat so he would have an easier time getting in and out of the car. She jumped quickly into the backseat before the moment could turn into more conflict. She leaned back against the seat and tried to relax a little. It wouldn't help Alice if she couldn't calm down and think clearly.

They made the short ride to the inn in silence, each of them deep in their own thoughts. Annie spotted the lanky prop master standing on the front steps of the inn, leaning against one of the columns. She hopped out of the car almost before it came to a complete stop.

"Samuel," she called as she hurried up the steps. "I am so glad we found you."

Samuel blushed slightly and dropped a cigarette onto the steps and crushed it with his foot. Then he picked up the butt. "You caught me," he said sheepishly. "I've been try-ing to quit, but ..." He let the sentence fade away, and then shrugged and rubbed the fading scrapes on his face.

"You'll be glad when you finally do," Annie said. "But right now, I really need your help."

Samuel smiled. "Sure, what can I do for you? You got your suitcases back, didn't you?"

"Actually I did," Annie said. "That's part of the problem."

As she spoke, Ian and Jim climbed the steps behind her and stood next to her. Samuel looked from one tall frowning man to another. "Hey," he said, "I'm not in trouble with you guys, am I?"

"No, of course not," Ian said, forcing a smile. Jim kept the same grim stare, not even trying to put the young prop master at ease.

"We need to borrow one of the other suitcases," Annie said. "The little valise that looks like mine. Someone really … needs it, and mine is out of town right now. It's really important, or I wouldn't ask."

Samuel shrugged, still looking a little confused. "Sure, no problem. We won't be using the cases for any of the other scenes. You're welcome to it. Come on up to the room. I'm cohabiting with the props right now. This movie has turned into a prop master's nightmare with the unexpected change in location and the way they keep changing scenes. Just when I think I have all the stuff we're going to need, they make a change, and I'm back to haunting thrift shops." He led the way into the inn and started up the long stairs to his room.

"Jim," Annie said, laying a gentle hand on her friend's arm, "why don't you wait down here? If his room is crowded with junk, it'll be easier with fewer of us. Ian and I have both seen the case." She knew Jim would have trouble with the long flight of stairs and didn't want to wear her friend out. They might need him later.

Jim nodded. "I'll go warm my old bones by the fire."

Annie hurried up the stairs to catch up with Samuel and Ian. They reached the young man's room and waited while the prop master opened the door with an old-fashioned metal key. Maplehurst Inn liked to keep things as vintage as possible.

Inside Samuel's room, suitcases and small bits of bric-a-brac covered every surface and were piled in every corner. He swept an arm out toward the mess. "Have at it," he said. "If you can find the case you need, you're welcome to it. In fact, you can borrow ten or fifteen if you want. Then I might be able to put my feet on the floor when I get up in the morning."

Annie and Ian looked over the piles carefully.

"Is this it?" Annie turned and found Ian holding up a small brown suitcase with brass trim.

"No," Annie said. "It looks a lot like that, but the trim is caramel-color leather with silver caps on the corners."

They poked at piles a bit longer until Annie caught sight of chocolate-color leather peeking out from under the edge of the bed. She slipped through the piles, glad for the practice she'd had slipping through the attic at Grey Gables. Then she tugged the bag out from under the bed. "This is it! It looks exactly like mine."

"Oh, I wonder how that got under there," Samuel said, scratching his head. "This room is just a lost world. You're welcome to use it, but as I remember, that one is locked shut. I didn't bother forcing the locks, but I don't have a key. Will that matter?"

"It shouldn't," Annie said. "We don't need to get inside it." Then she took a deep breath. "It's possible something could ... um ... happen to it while we're using it."

"Happen to it?" Samuel echoed.

"Like we could lose it."

"Oh," Samuel looked at them in confusion. "Well, I have the receipt around here somewhere for what I paid for it at the thrift shop. I guess if something happened to it, you could just reimburse the movie company. Like I said, the director promised me that we're done with the suitcase scenes."

"Oh, good. That's great then." Annie impulsively kissed the young man on the cheek. "You've been a huge help."

Samuel's look of bewilderment hadn't changed much. "Good. Glad to help. Have fun with it."

Ian thanked Samuel again, and then ushered Annie out of the room. "Now we just have to wait for the kidnapper to call again," he said.

"Yes," Annie said bleakly. "That's all we have to do. Oh, poor Alice. She must be so scared. I hope she's warm enough. What if he crammed her into a car trunk? They do that all the time on television."

Ian put his arm around Annie, giving her a brief hug. "This isn't television. She'll be fine. We'll get her back."

"I know. We have to."

They drove back to Grey Gables in the same heavy silence as the trip to the inn. Annie's stomach knotted up at the thought of Alice being held somewhere by the same person who tried to force them off the road. Over and over she ran through the mugging and the frightening struggle on the highway, trying to remember some clue that would help them go find Alice right now! But each time, she came up empty. They just had to wait for the kidnapper.

At Grey Gables, Jim and Ian both hustled Annie onto the sofa in the front room.

"I'll go get you a cup of tea," Jim said.

"Oh no." Annie began to rise. "You're my guest. You shouldn't be waiting on me."

Jim held up his hand. "These are extreme circumstances, and you're shaking like a leaf. I know my way around a kitchen pretty well. I'm sure the mayor wouldn't mind if I left the two of you alone for a little while." Jim shifted his eyes to Ian briefly, and then thumped out of the room.

Ian sat on the sofa beside Annie. He took her icy fingers between his two large warm hands. "I need to go and call Chief Edwards," he said. "If I don't keep him apprised of the situation, he's not going to be willing to stay away. It took some serious talking to get him to go along with this in the first place. It'll just take me a couple minutes."

Annie nodded. Ian let go of her hands and stood up. She had to fight the urge to call him back. She was just so scared for her friend. Reconnecting with Alice after moving to Stony Point had been the first step in really feeling at home in the village. She'd had some tight moments with the mysteries they kept falling into, but nothing had scared her as much as this, nor made her feel as helpless.

Annie jumped as a warm bundle of cat was piled into her arms. She looked up in surprise at Ian. "Boots will help warm you up until I'm done on the phone," Ian said with a smile.

Annie smiled gratefully and hugged Boots close to her. Boots seemed to sense Annie's worry because the cat put up with the squeezing stoically and even purred. The warm rumble began to unknot the fear in Annie's stomach a bit.

At the soft thump of Jim's cane, Annie was pulled back into the moment again. She gave herself a mental shake. She couldn't keep drifting away like that. She needed to stay focused, though she wasn't sure what she should focus on.

In one hand, Jim carried a small wooden tray Annie kept in the cupboard. On it he balanced three steaming mugs and a plate of cookies. He set the tray on the coffee table in front of Annie and then sat beside her on the sofa.

"If I know my girl," Jim said, squeezing Annie's hand, "she's giving that kidnapper heck. You never know, she might show up here with the kidnapper tied up in Princessa necklace chains."

Annie smiled a little. She could clearly imagine Alice giving the kidnapper plenty of trouble, but was that good or bad? What if the kidnapper had a gun? What if he'd already hurt Alice for being hard to handle? Annie hugged Boots a little tighter until the cat protested with a cranky meow and a lot of wiggling.

"Sorry Boots," Annie said, setting the cat on her lap. Boots gave her an accusing glare, and then settled into Annie's lap.

Ian joined them minutes later. "The chief is still not happy, but he promised to keep away from the house. As soon as we know the drop plans though, I have to pass along the information."

"So he can spook the kidnapper?" Jim demanded, straightening up to his full height as if he were getting ready to fight over this.

"Chief Edwards is better than that," Ian said quietly. "We need to trust him."

"The only person I trust with Alice is me," Jim said.

Annie patted Jim's arm. "I believe Chief Edwards won't do anything to endanger Alice," she said. "He's a good man too."

Jim made a sound that sounded a lot like a growl and paced across the room. "I'm not really good at waiting," he said. "It's frustrating not to have something to go and do about this. I feel like I should be out looking for her. Or throttling someone."

"Where would you look?" Ian asked. "Who would you throttle?"

Jim's shoulders slumped. "I don't know. You know the area, where would you hide someone if you were a kidnapper?"

"Well, if he's still driving the SUV he used to force Alice and Annie off the road, he could just keep her in the vehicle," Ian said thoughtfully. "Though if this is someone local, he could also have simply taken her to his house. Chief Edwards could begin a house-to-house search, but that would be likely to tip off the kidnapper."

"What about the DMV?" Jim said. "Can the police track down local SUVs? How many can there be?"

"Actually it's the BMV in Maine," Ian said. "The Bureau of Motor Vehicles. Heavy four-wheel drive vehicles are fairly popular up here with all the snow, but that is one of the things the chief said he's checking out." He looked at the other man's lined face in sympathy. "Waiting is hard on us all."

Jim forced a smile. "I guess we need to look for a way to pass the time. Anyone want to play cards?"

"Sure," Ian said. "But not for money. I have the feeling you'd soon have my house, my car, and my dog."

"I could use a good dog," Jim said. He chuckled but the normally warm sound was forced.

Annie got up to look for a deck of cards. She was pretty sure she'd seen a deck in the junk drawer in the kitchen. She looked at the bright sun shining in the kitchen window and groaned. Midnight seemed so far away. How would she survive the wait? Then she felt the chill in the pit of her stomach. Could Alice survive the wait?

Time passed as slowly as Annie had expected. Ian and Jim seemed to bond a bit over the few rounds of gin rummy they played. She made sandwiches and heated soup for them all, but no one had much appetite. Normally night rushed at Annie in the New England winter, but today she couldn't see the end of daylight fast enough to suit her.

Finally, when she was almost sure the waiting would make her scream, a ringtone from her pocket startled her. She put it on speakerphone and set it on the table with trembling hands.

"I saw the mayor at your house," the raspy whisper said. "Alice says that's your boyfriend. Who's the old guy with the cane?"

"I'm Alice's boyfriend," Jim roared. "And if you hurt her, I'll kill you."

"Calm down, old man," the whisper sounded amused. "I can't believe that hot redhead can't do better than some old cripple. She's quite a firecracker."

Ian put a restraining hand on Jim's arm and leaned close

to whisper in his ear. Jim settled back down, though his face stayed flush.

"How do I know you haven't hurt Alice?" Annie asked.

"She's well enough to tell me the mayor is your boyfriend," the kidnapper said.

"But not well enough to identify her own friend?" Annie responded. "I am not doing another thing until I hear Alice's voice and know she's all right. Not one thing."

"You'll do what I tell you," the man snarled, his voice raising above a whisper for the first time. A nudge of recognition pushed at Annie, but it was too fleeting to catch hold.

"Let me talk to her." Annie was proud of how calm and even her voice sounded. She wasn't sure how she'd managed it since her hands were shaking.

The phone fell silent for a few minutes, and then they heard someone cough and Alice said, "Annie? I'm OK."

~13~

Annie felt faint with relief.

"Alice?" Jim shouted, lunging toward the phone.

"See, she's fine," the kidnapper was back to whispering. "And we're done with the chitchat. You're going to bring the suitcase to the small beach across and below you. Put it in the shaved-ice stand. You'll find directions there for collecting your friend. I want you to drop the case exactly at midnight. And if I see anyone but you, I'll cut Red's head off. So you better keep all the boyfriends away."

"I'll do as you say," Annie said. "This suitcase doesn't mean anything to me. All I want is Alice."

"Good attitude. I'll see you shortly."

The call dropped, and Annie looked at her watch. It was exactly eleven-thirty. She only needed a few minutes to drive down to the beach, which still left them with time on their hands.

"I'll call the chief," Ian said.

Jim reached out and caught Ian's arm. "Are you sure that's a good idea. I don't want anything to mess this up."

"Nothing will," Ian said. "I'm sure."

Jim slumped again, taking his hand away. "I hate this."

"Me too," Annie said, and she gave the grizzled man a quick hug. Ian frowned slightly at that but didn't comment. Instead, he stepped slightly away from them into the corner of the room where he couldn't be seen from any of the   windows, just in case the kidnapper was watching them somehow. Then Ian pulled out his cellphone and spoke quietly into it for a few minutes.

Annie stood and began gathering up the half-eaten sandwiches and the soup mugs. She just needed something to do with her hands. Jim followed her into the kitchen.

"I hope I haven't made this any harder on you," he said gently.

"No, you and Ian have made it easier," she said. "I would have gone crazy if I had had to do this alone."

"I don't like the idea of you going to the beach alone," Jim said.

"I'm not crazy about it either," Annie said, "but it's what the kidnapper ordered."

They turned as Ian walked into the room. "I could slump down in the backseat," he said. "He wouldn't see me."

"Unless he's watching the house now," Annie said, "and he sees you get into the car. Plus, you're too tall to hide in the backseat."

"You'd be surprised at what I can do," Ian said. "Look, Jim and I are going to have to move our cars anyway to let you out. I could make the transfer then. It's dark out, and you don't have any kind of decent security lights." He paused for a moment. "We need to do something about that, by the way. But this time it'll work in our favor. I'll get in the backseat as you get in the front." When Annie started to speak, he held up a hand. "I'm not letting you go alone."

Annie chewed her lip. She didn't want to go alone, but she didn't want to risk Alice either.

"Ian's right," Jim said. "You need someone there in case things go wrong. I'll create a distraction just as you get in the car. That should draw the kidnapper's eye to me if he's watching."

"What kind of distraction?"

"You'll see." Jim's eyes sparkled with mischief, and Annie was glad to see it. Clearly Jim needed to feel like he was doing something to help too.

All three of them dressed back in their coats and hats. Annie picked up the small valise, and they headed out into the cold again. Ian backed up his car and pulled it onto Annie's lawn. With the coming of night, the wet ground had frozen hard again, so the tires didn't sink and there was no danger of the cars getting stuck. Jim pulled his car up beside Ian's.

Then both men got out of the cars, and Annie saw the flair of light from the cars' interiors lighting them up brightly. They quickly closed their doors. As soon as it was dark again, Jim shouted, "Hey, you're too close to my car!"

"I parked first," Ian shouted back. "You're too close to my car!"

"Look, I'm tired of you thinking you know everything just because you're mayor!"

Annie realized this must be the distraction Jim promised. "I don't have time for any more of this. I'm leaving!" she shouted into the darkness. "You two need to grow up!" She felt a twinge of guilt at what she said, but hoped her friends knew she was just acting for the kidnapper's benefit.

"Grow up?" Jim roared. "I can't believe the nerve of you and that swishy mayor!" He continued to rant, his voice climbing with each sentence.

Annie stomped to her car and swung the door open, shouting something that was drowned out by Jim's booming voice. She heard the soft sound of the back door closing on the car, and she climbed in and slammed her door hard.

"Ian?" she whispered.

"I'm ready to go."

She pulled out of the drive, leaving Jim ranting at a mayor who was no longer there. Annie drove slowly down the road, keenly aware that the same cold that had saved her lawn from the tires of the two cars was also likely to have left invisible ice on the highway.

What if the kidnapper decided to skip the meeting on the beach and just run her off the road to get the valise? He had practice at that! Her fingers tightened on the wheel as she crept around each curve.

Finally they reached the parking lot of the small beach. "We're here," Annie said. "I'm going to go drop the valise."

"I'll get out when you do," Ian said. "But don't worry. I'll make sure he doesn't see me. Just make sure you make some kind of noise."

Annie nodded and opened her door. She stood beside it, bathed in the light from the interior. "If you're out there," she shouted, "I'm here! I'm taking the case to the stand."

Then she heard the soft sound of the back door and slammed her own door. She didn't look for Ian in the dark, but headed straight across the rocky sand instead. The wind off the water was vicious, making Annie's eyes water as it struck her face.

The packed sand under her feet was mostly level, but she had to dodge rocks as she walked. They were sharp, and she knew that if she stepped on one, she could end up with a turned ankle. That wouldn't help anyone. She finally reached the shaved-ice stand and saw an envelope taped to one of the upright posts of the stand. The white of the paper shone in the darkness. Annie pulled the envelope free and dropped the valise into the stand. Then she turned and looked around.

She saw no sign of movement anywhere on the beach or in the surrounding rocks. The cliff side that rose up along one side of the small beach seemed particularly ominous in the darkness, but she saw nothing move in that direction either.

Annie walked carefully back to the car, she kept an eye out for Ian but didn't see him until it was time to open the car and get in. She spotted him huddled close to the Malibu.

She pulled open the front door and got in. She left the door open while she tore open the envelope. The note was just three words cut from newsprint and glued to the paper.

"Old Seaman's Rest," she whispered. "I don't know where that is."

"Go ahead and slam your door on three," Ian's voice spoke from the backseat. "One, two ... three!"

On three, both the front and back door slammed shut.

"Old Seaman's Rest is down Grand Avenue, past pretty much everything," Ian said.

Annie drove carefully, though not nearly as slowly as she had before. As they passed the various businesses and the Ocean View Assisted Living Center, Ian finally sat up in the backseat. "It's not far now," he said.

Annie nodded, blinking back tears. "Please let Alice be safe," she prayed, her lips forming the words silently.

Ian pointed just ahead where an old building set back off the road a bit. All the windows were boarded up. "The Historical Society has talked about doing something with this once or twice," he said. "That's why it hasn't been torn down."

Annie just nodded again, not trusting her voice to come out steady. She pulled up close to the building, but she left the car running and the headlights on for light. Then she pulled a flashlight out of the glove box.

They got out of the car together, and Ian put an arm around Annie. "We have to be careful in there," Ian said. "I haven't been inside in years, but I don't think it's too stable. Alice won't be helped if you fall through the floor and into the cellar."

Annie nodded, but walked quickly to the door. She saw that a hasp and padlock had once kept the door closed. Now the padlock lay on the ground where it had been cut off the hasp.

"Let me go first," Ian insisted. "He took the flashlight from Annie's shaking fingers and held her hand. Then he stepped inside with her directly behind him.

"Alice?" Annie called out.

They heard some muffled sounds and loud thumping. Ian swept the room with his light. Alice lay on the floor close to the far wall. She had been bound to a chair with duct tape but had clearly turned herself over. One of the chair's legs was broken, probably from Alice's boot heel slamming into it.

Ian and Annie rushed over. Annie gently pulled a strip of duct tape from Alice's mouth. "Are you all right?" she asked as Ian pulled out a penknife and began cutting her free of the chair.

"Sure," Alice's voice sounded rusty. "I could use a drink of water though."

"I'm sorry," Annie said. "I didn't think to bring any."

"That's OK," Alice said with a grin that looked wonderful to Annie. "I try not to complain about rescues."

As soon as Ian had Alice free, they helped her to her feet. Alice was a little wobbly. "My feet went to sleep," Alice said. "Actually, my everything went to sleep. I do not recommend spending any time tied to a chair."

Annie laughed shakily and hugged her friend. "I was so scared."

"I wasn't," Alice said. "I knew you'd come get me. Besides, that kidnapper didn't strike me as the killing sort."

"Did you get a good look at him?" Ian asked as they helped her across the room toward the door

Alice shook her head. "He had a ski mask on. But you could look for a guy with seriously banged up shins. My boots have some killer heels. And I bit him on the hand too. I can guarantee that left a mark."

Ian smiled. "Sounds like the man is probably glad to be rescued from you."

"Yeah, I wish I'd done more damage. He used that stupid SUV to force me off the road again. Only this time he actually did it. You should see my car!"

"Chief Edwards found it," Ian said. "He said it looked pretty banged up."

"You didn't tell me that," Annie said.

"You were worried enough," Ian said. "And apparently Alice drove it into a tree."

"It was that SUV," Alice muttered. "Did Chief Edwards catch the guy yet?"

"I don't know," Ian said. "He hasn't called. Annie only just dropped off the valise."

"The valise?" Alice yelped. "He just wanted that suitcase? He wrecked my car and kidnapped me for a stupid empty suitcase?"

Annie shrugged. "Apparently, but you know Vanessa has mine. I borrowed the other one from the prop department."

They reached the car. By then Alice was able to walk without so much wobbling. They drove quickly back to Grey Gables.

"Jim will certainly be glad to see you," Ian said.

"Jim?" Alice echoed, her face lighting up. "Jim Parker? He's here?"

"Didn't you hear him on the phone?" Annie asked.

"I didn't talk on the phone," Alice said.

"But I heard your voice."

"The kidnapper had me talk into a tape recorder before he left me tied up this morning," Alice said. "I've been trying to get loose ever since. That guy sure loves duct tape."

"How did the kidnapper know that building was the Old Seaman's Rest?" Annie asked.

"He asked me what to call it," Alice said.

"Did you also tell him Ian was my boyfriend?" Annie asked.

Alice shook her head. "Ian didn't come up in our brief

conversation. The guy wasn't all that chatty. Now tell me about Jim. Is he OK?"

"Jim showed up early this afternoon," Annie said. "He's waiting for us at Grey Gables. He's been beside himself with worry." She cut her eyes toward her friend and saw Alice run her fingers through her hair and wipe at her dirty face. "He'll think you look great."

They pulled up in front of Grey Gables as the front door flew open and Jim lurched across the porch. Alice jumped out of the car the second Annie shut it off. Her friend ran for the porch without a thought toward the icy steps.

"Be careful," Annie yelled, just as Alice slipped on the top step and tumbled into Jim's arms.

"I got you, Red," Jim said. Then he kissed her.

Annie and Ian turned away to give them a moment of privacy, but it was too cold to let them have any prolonged greeting. Annie wanted to be inside.

"I hate to break things up, but Annie is shivering," Ian called.

Alice slipped her arm through Jim's and tugged him toward the house. "I didn't notice the cold," she said. "Sorry, Annie."

"I might not have noticed the cold in your situation either," Annie said.

"We could try it and see," Ian suggested.

Annie looked at him in shock, and then punched his arm lightly when she saw the twinkle in his eyes. "No teasing," she said. "I've had a hard day."

"OK, no teasing," Ian agreed. He took Annie's hand, and they walked into the house behind their friends.

~14~

"Why didn't you let me know you were coming here?" Alice asked Jim as they settled on the sofa in the living room. Annie and Ian gave them some privacy by heading to the kitchen to get some hot cocoa since everyone but Jim was chilled to the bone. "How long are you staying? I thought you were in Arizona."

"I wrapped up there last week," he said. "I sent you a letter. I sent you a whole package about it. I understand it had a little accident in the mail." He laughed. "I included some photos of the ghost town so you could see it and a CD with the playlist I got as a joke from someone. He called it "I'm coming for you" and said it was music to photograph ghosts by."

Alice laughed until tears streamed down her face. "I got that package," she finally gasped, "but it was torn up. All I got was the CD with 'I'm coming for you,' scrawled on it."

"Scrawled?" Jim feigned insult. "You could read it couldn't you?"

"I thought someone was sending me a warning," Alice said. "We were convinced I had a crazy stalker."

"You do," Jim said, putting an arm around Alice and pulling her close. "I'm crazy about you, and I'd stalk you anywhere."

Alice shook her head and gave him a playful shove. "Now it's getting thick. So it was your package that scared me half to death. One mystery solved. Tell me, how long are you staying?"

"Trying to get rid of me already?" he asked.

"Not a bit," she said. "Just wondering if I need to buy you a Christmas present."

"Afraid so," he said. "I'm here until New Year's Day, but then I have to leave for a shoot at an abandoned state mental hospital in Connecticut. They've sold it to some developer, and I'm getting the last photos before it's torn down. I was hoping you'd come with me. There might be ghosts."

"Ghosts?" Alice said.

Jim shrugged. "So they say. It also has creepy tunnels, peeling paint, mold, and other disgusting things."

"Tunnels? In a hospital?" Alice said.

"It's more than just a hospital," Jim said. "It was practically a little town. There are all these different buildings, including a church. And old houses where the staff lived. The tunnels join some of the buildings for moving ... well, you know, things ... in the dead of night. You'll love it."

"You do know how to sweet-talk a lady," Alice said. "I'll think about it. But before I decide about any trips with you, we need to solve the current mystery."

"I'm in," Jim said. "I'm not letting you out of my sight."

Just then Annie and Ian walked back into the room with thick mugs of hot chocolate. Annie handed one to Alice. "Three marshmallows," she said. "Just the way you like it."

"Wow, I could get used to this treatment," Alice said.

A muffled ringtone sounded and Annie fumbled for her pocket until she realized it was Ian's phone. "Chief Edwards," Ian said as he looked at the phone. He backed away from the group a bit and took the call.

Annie watched Ian's face closely, hoping for good news. She wanted this mystery to be over right now. The conversation seemed to go on for a while, but Ian finally returned to the group. He walked back toward the sofa with the weight of all eyes upon him.

"The chief says the man got away. They saw him go after the valise, but apparently he tripped a series of small explosions and escaped in the confusion. The chief said the guy was very athletic."

"I don't suppose the guy was limping?" Alice said hopefully. "I was hoping I'd cracked a bone kicking him."

"Chief Edwards didn't mention any limping."

"Explosions," Annie whispered in horror. She looked around at her friends. "So this guy is some kind of bomb expert too?"

"Apparently they were fairly small explosions," Ian said. "The chief said they looked like the kind of thing you'd find in a movie. Carefully set for the most bang with the least risk."

"Does the chief think this guy is with the movie?" Alice asked.

"He might be," Ian said. "With the bombs and the guy being an athlete, he might be a stuntman. I didn't think this was the kind of movie to need stunts though. It's supposed to be more of a mushy sentimental story."

"Is the chief going to question the movie people?" Jim asked.

"He's planning to."

Annie trembled at the thought of the man still being on

the lam. Alice looked her way and then stood to give her a hug. "Hey, the guy got what he wanted, right?" Alice said. "So he shouldn't have any more interest in us."

"But he didn't exactly get what he wanted," Annie said. "My suitcase is still with Vanessa. The one he got was from the movie."

"Hopefully, it won't make a difference," Alice said.

"Is this a valuable piece of luggage?" Jim asked. "It didn't look like much to me."

"It isn't," Annie said. "None of this makes any sense."

"Mysteries don't," Jim said. "Not until you get all the pieces."

"I don't want any more pieces of this one," Annie said. "I just want a nice peaceful Christmas." With that, she was suddenly hit with how exhausted she really was, and she tried to fight back a huge yawn with little success.

"You look beat, and I know I am," Alice said. "Jim and I will head out now. I've got plenty of room at my place for one slightly rumpled photographer."

"Rumpled?" Jim protested. "At least I don't have spiderwebs in my hair."

Alice's hands flew to her hair. "Where?" she asked. "Do you think there are spiders too? I hate spiders."

"I'll check you over when we get next door," Jim said laughing. "Let's go. Like I said, I'm not letting you out of my sight."

After Alice and Jim left, Annie began to gather up the things, but her feet nearly dragged as she walked. Ian took the mugs from her. "I'll clean up before I leave," he said. "And I'll check all the locks on the windows and doors. You go on to bed before you fall down."

Annie considered protesting, but she just didn't have the energy. She smiled gratefully and scooped up Boots before heading for her room. She fell asleep listening to the comforting sounds of Ian moving through the house.

Annie woke to a shadowy room and a chubby cat walking up and down on top of the covers. "OK, Boots," she said. "I'm getting up."

Boots meowed, and then settled down on Annie's pillow as Annie sat up and slipped into her robe. "Today has to go better than yesterday, right?" she asked Boots.

Boots merely blinked at her as if it were Annie interrupting the cat's rest.

Anne smiled and shook her head. When she opened the bedroom door, she nearly tripped over a body wrapped in a blanket and laying on the floor.

Annie shrieked, and the body jerked into a sitting position and fought itself loose of the blanket. Suddenly, Ian's head appeared, his short salt-and-pepper hair as rumpled as Annie had ever seen it.

"Ian," Annie said, "what are you doing on the floor?"

Ian stood, looking sheepish. "I intended to be up before you. After I straightened up last night, I just couldn't leave you alone. Not with that kidnapper still loose. So I thought I would stay."

"On the floor?" Annie said. "There's a perfectly good guest room right down the hall."

Ian nodded. "But I just felt better knowing anyone wanting to get to you would have to get past me."

"Or fall over you," Annie said. "What if I'd had to go to

the bathroom in the night? I could have hurt you."

Ian looked even more sheepish. "It was late. I didn't say I'd thought it all the way through."

Finally Annie smiled. "Well, I appreciate the gesture. And for that, I'll fix you some breakfast."

Ian raised the sleeve of his shirt to look at his watch. "I don't think there's time," he said. "I promised to deliver you to Chief Edwards's office this morning. How about I treat you to breakfast at the diner instead, after we visit the chief's office?"

"That's fine, but you'll have to give me a few minutes to shower and change."

"No problem."

Annie looked over Ian's rumpled clothes. "Do we need to stop by your house? Your clothes look a bit like you slept in them."

Ian shook his head. "At least it's not a workday," he said. "I'll go home and change after we get some breakfast."

Annie hurried off to the bathroom for a quick shower. Then she dressed in a pair of lined wool pants in a rich burgundy topped by a whisper-soft vanilla sweater. She ran a brush through her hair but left it loose. She'd pull a hat on over it.

Boots hopped off the bed to meow and wind her way through Annie's legs as soon as Annie got dressed. "Thanks, Boots," Annie said. "The gray cat hair will complement these pants nicely."

Boots just rubbed harder, so Annie danced around the cat, trying not to trip, and headed for the kitchen to serve the cat a princess's breakfast.

"We should take separate cars," Ian said, "since we'll be parting company in town. Do you have your cellphone? I want you to call me if you notice anyone suspicious following you."

"Don't worry," Annie said. "I'm not feeling overly brave today. At the first sign of anything, I'll yell."

When they arrived at Chief Edwards's office, the chief stood and took Annie's hand. "I've never met anyone who is quite such a magnet for trouble as you are, Mrs. Dawson."

"I'm not sure about that," Ian said as he crossed his arms. "Alice McFarlane may come in a close second."

The chief chuckled and nodded. "Alice is coming in later to give a statement. I called her this morning and got quite an earful from that photographer she's taken up with."

"We're all a bit on edge from this," Annie said.

"Well, I've heard about the events of the past few days from Ian," Chief Edwards said as he gestured at a chair for Annie. "But I was hoping you could fill me in directly."

Annie told the chief about the attempted mugging in the parking lot at the waterfront. As she spoke, she was amazed that that was only a couple of days earlier. It felt like much longer. She went on to describe the attempt to run Alice's car off the road, and then everything she knew about the kidnapping.

"Ian told me about some package Alice had gotten also," Chief Edwards said. "Did you see it?"

Annie smiled. "Yes, but it turns out that's not related. It's a case of mistaken identity for the poor package. It was actually from Jim, but was so damaged in transit that it looked much more sinister than it was."

The chief nodded. "It's good to have one part of a mystery

solved. As you know, we had the beach staked out. We saw you drop the valise, and we watched for the pick up. But we had not seen the preparations the kidnapper made beforehand. Once the explosions started, it threw everything into chaos, and the man escaped with the valise. Do you have any idea why the man wanted that particular suitcase?"

Annie shook her head. "It isn't anything special. We looked it over closely after the man tried to steal it the first time. I have no idea why anyone would want it."

"It's my understanding that the case the man got wasn't the one he wanted? Maybe you could bring the original case in and let my men look at it?"

Annie nodded. "Sure, I'll do that."

They chatted for a few more minutes as Annie went over every detail she remembered about the man during the mugging attempt. They were scant enough. The man was taller than her, but she really didn't know much else.

Finally, she and Ian thanked the chief and left. As they walked across the Town Square, Ian said, "This is where they're shooting the last scene here in Stony Point tomorrow."

Annie nodded. "Do you know what the scene is supposed to be about?"

"The town is upset about something Logan Lariby's character has done," Ian said. "I believe it's going to be Logan's big scene when he saves the day and makes his dad proud of him."

"Vanessa will like that," Annie said. "She's quite taken with that young man."

"He seems very polite," Ian answered. "I'm sorry I haven't met Matt Rusher. I've always enjoyed his other movies where things blow up."

Annie shook her head. "Well, we had the explosions last night apparently, even if they weren't in the movie."

"And I missed them."

"But you were playing the action hero at the time," Annie said, smiling up at him.

Ian laughed. "I don't think I'm really cut out to be an action hero."

"I don't know." Annie stopped and made a big show of looking at his profile. "You have the jawline for it. Very rugged."

Ian just shook his head with a smile as they crossed the street and slipped into the diner. Peggy rushed over to meet them with a bright smile. "Alice is here with Jim. I didn't know he was back in town," she said.

"It was a surprise," Annie said.

"They make such a cute couple," Peggy said. Annie knew Peggy loved the whole idea of romance. Most of the Hook and Needle Club members did. Annie was just glad to see all that interest turned in the direction of someone else for a change. Usually she was the one getting teased about Ian.

"Do you want to join them?" Peggy asked nodding toward the table where Alice and Jim sat side by side.

"No," Ian said quickly. "We'll let them have their privacy."

Peggy led them to a small table. She glanced back toward the kitchen where her boss was watching her pointedly. "He's such a grouch this morning," Peggy whispered as she poured them each a cup of coffee from the pot she seemed always to have in one hand. "What would you two like?"

"My usual," Ian said. "I'm not feeling very adventurous this morning."

"How about you?" Peggy asked. "We have some gorgeous banana nut muffins that just came out of the oven. Still warm and huge."

"You sold me," Annie said.

As Peggy hurried away, Annie smiled at Ian. "You were awfully eager not to join Jim and Alice. You know, he really is a very nice guy."

Ian looked at her over the rim of his coffee mug. "Maybe I just wanted to be alone with you."

"Sure."

"OK, I think Jim and I just rub each other the wrong way," Ian said.

"Maybe you are too much alike," Annie suggested.

Ian's eyes widened. "We are nothing alike. He leaves the woman he appears to care about so he can traipse all over the country. He has no sense of home or stability. And he actually likes it that Alice takes crazy risks."

"But he's also very protective of her," Annie said. "And loyal. And charming."

Ian harrumphed. "So, did you ever figure out what to give your son-in-law for Christmas?"

"Smooth subject change, Mr. Mayor."

Ian shrugged. "It's the politician in me. So did you?"

"Yes, and you inspired it," she said.

"How did I do that?"

"When you suggested a book. I liked the idea of a book, but I needed to give him the whole library. I just couldn't choose."

"How did that help you?"

"I bought him one of those electronic book readers,"

she said. "It came with two free book downloads. After that, I'm sure he'll fill it up with his own books." She sat back in the seat with a huge smile.

"Sounds like a great idea," Ian said. "So, one problem solved."

"I wish they were all so easy," Annie said.

~ 15 ~

Annie and Ian ate the rest of their breakfast chatting lightly about Christmas and the difficulties in gift giving. Finally Annie sat back in her chair with an empty plate and a contented stomach.

"I think I'll stop by A Stitch in Time and see how Vanessa is enjoying her weekend," Annie said. "I still worry a little about her having that suitcase."

Ian raised his eyebrows. "Is Mary Beth still opening on Sunday?"

"She does for the Christmas season," Annie said, "but only for a couple hours. I need to get over there while they're still open. Thank you for everything last night and this morning."

"I wouldn't have wanted to be left out of it," he said.

She reached out and patted his wrinkled shirt sleeve. Then she paid her check and looked toward Alice's table. She wondered if she should stop and say hello, but decided against it. Her two friends didn't look as if they needed more company. Annie braced herself and stepped back out into the cold.

She looked up at the sky as she walked the short distance to A Stitch in Time. The clouds looked like a gray washboard. "Looks like more snow," Annie muttered with a shiver.

As always, A Stitch in Time greeted her with a whoosh of warmth as she opened the door. Kate looked up from the counter and smiled. She looked especially pretty in the long crocheted sweater dress she wore.

"Hi, Annie," Kate said. "I missed you at church."

Annie sighed. "I was sorry to miss it. I slept in, and even Boots couldn't get me out of bed. But I'll be there next week, even if I have to get a sled-dog team."

"Oh, you noticed our snow clouds?" Kate asked. "I've been listening to the weather report. Our little warm snap seems to be over. They're warning about a possible blizzard next week."

"That would make it tough on the moviemakers, I'd imagine."

Kate shrugged. "That's all right with me. Vanessa could talk about something else for a while that way."

"Speaking of your lovely daughter, has she enjoyed her trip?"

Kate nodded. "She called from the lodge last night. They got some skiing in yesterday and are planning some more tonight. She's going to be getting home pretty late, but I'm glad she got this chance. Harry's parents are everything I could ask for in grandparents for Vanessa."

"That's good," Annie said. She knew that Harry wasn't everything Kate could hope for in a dad for Vanessa. In some ways, Harry could be a kid himself.

"Oh, I have something for you," Kate said. "I totally forgot when you were in here before. Hold on while I find it." Kate turned and hurried into the back room.

Annie wondered what Kate could mean. She knew she

wasn't expecting any kind of yarn order. Then Kate came out carrying the brown valise. "Vanessa didn't take it after all," Kate said. "Apparently it's locked, and she didn't want to force it open. So she couldn't use it."

"That doesn't make sense," Annie said. "The locks were broken. I'm sure of it. They couldn't have locked." She took the case from Kate and looked it over carefully. Then she realized the case in her hands wasn't hers.

"Oh, dear, this isn't my valise," she said. "They must have been switched in the props department. I had their case on the second day of filming."

"Oh well, that would explain the locks then," Kate said. "Vanessa wondered why you loaned her a locked case."

"I'd imagine," Annie said. "Well, good. I can return this to the prop master." Then she felt a rush of relief. This meant the case they'd given the kidnapper the night before really was hers. The man actually got what he wanted. They might not have solved the mystery, but at least the man had no more reason to come after her.

She considered pouring out the story to Kate, but then she stopped. She'd have to tell it all at the Hook and Needle Club meeting on Tuesday. She might as well save it for then. She chatted with Kate a bit longer about Christmas, and then carried the valise out to her car.

She considered stopping by Maplehurst Inn and getting rid of the valise right away. She found it made her nervous sitting on the seat beside her. Then she shook her head.

That's just silly, she told herself sternly.

Annie pulled up in front of Grey Gables and hurried up onto the porch, eager to get out of the cold. As she pulled out her keys, she saw the front door was slightly ajar. Annie just stared at the small crack, frozen. She was sure they hadn't left the door open. Ian was too careful for that.

Annie backed up slowly, feeling backward with her foot to avoid tripping on the stairs. Still, she nearly tumbled backward when she heard someone shout her name. Catching herself at the last second, she turned to see Alice running across the lawn from the carriage house. "Annie!" she called. "Someone's been in my house. It's ransacked!"

"Someone's been in Grey Gables too!" Annie exclaimed. "The door is open. I haven't been inside."

Alice stood beside her, and they looked up toward the door as Jim caught up to them. "Are we staring at the door for a reason?" he asked, his voice slightly breathy.

"It's open a little," Annie said. "I'm scared to go in."

"Well, I'm not," Jim said firmly. "I'd like to get my hands on this guy. I may not be fast, but I'd still show him something." He climbed the steps and pushed the door open.

A gray streak flashed past his legs.

"Boots!" Annie called, but the cat ran right past her as well. Annie watched Boots race up the nearest tree and peered down at them, her tail swishing.

"That certainly settles that," Alice said. "Someone's been inside."

Annie walked to the tree and reached up, calling Boots softly. The cat never moved. Her eyes stayed glued to the front door and her tail continued to twitch. "She's not going to give in," Annie said. "Maybe we should call the police."

"We certainly should," Alice said. "But I think we should also go in."

Jim didn't say anything. He just pushed the door the rest of the way open and walked in. Annie and Alice followed.

Annie groaned softly as she looked around her disheveled front room. The cushions had been pulled off the couch. Things were swept off shelves and dumped out of the drawers on the small end tables.

I don't understand, Annie thought. If he was looking for the valise, why would he look in drawers and under cushions? Maybe the valise isn't what he is after!

"Haven't we been here before?" Alice asked.

Annie forced a smile. It did seem like her house was searched a lot more often than could be considered strictly normal. "At least I'm getting better at putting things back in place," she said. "I better call the chief."

She pulled out her cellphone and dialed Chief Edwards's office. She wondered what it said about her that the chief of police was on her speed dial. The chief listened to her brief report. He said he'd be right over with some more officers to check out both houses. "You should go outside," the chief said, "just in case the man is still inside."

Annie passed the chief's recommendation on to her friends. "I don't think he's here," Jim said. "He's after something he thinks you have, Annie. I'm sure he searched this place first and Alice's after. He's long gone."

"And he's fast," Alice said. "How long have you been gone?"

"Hours," Annie said. "If he was watching the house, it didn't have to be that long. But this doesn't make any sense. He got the valise."

"Not the right one," Alice said.

"No, he did get the one he wanted." She explained the

mix-up with the cases and held up the valise she'd gotten from Kate. "This is the one from the props department. The one we left on the beach was mine."

Jim limped over and took the case from Annie. He looked at it carefully. "This one belongs to the movie people, and it's locked?"

"Yes," Annie said. "That's why Vanessa didn't take it."

"Maybe the guy never wanted your case," Jim said. "Maybe he thought you had this case during the movie shoot. This could be what he's been after all along."

"Who knows what's inside that," Alice said. "Diamonds, stocks, cash."

Annie thought about that for a moment, and then she remembered the one weird event that had started the whole mystery. The event they'd overlooked every time they thought about it. "Alice, do you remember when Stella told us she'd seen a car on the side of the road?"

Alice blinked at the change in subject. "Yeah."

"That was Samuel Ely's car," Annie said. "The casting director was riding with him and that's who Stella saw. Ms. Kensington told me someone had run them off the road."

"And Samuel is the prop master," Alice said.

"The man was after this case all the way back then," Annie said. "Before I even found my case in the attic."

"We should open it," Jim said.

"I don't know," Annie protested. "It's not technically mine, and I don't have the key. We'd have to force the locks."

"Didn't the prop master offer to sell it to you?" Jim asked. "Why would he care if you popped the locks. You could always just buy it." The photographer grinned, and then his eyes twinkled. "I'll pay for it if you want. We have the mystery right here in our hands; we have to open it."

"OK, let's open it," Annie agreed.

Jim carried the bag into the kitchen, and Annie moaned again at the destruction. The contents of all the kitchen drawers lay in a jumble on the floor. The counters were covered with canned goods swept from the cupboards.

Alice bent down and picked up a butter knife. "Can you pop locks with this?"

"In my sleep," Jim said. He carried the case to the table and used the knife Alice had handed him to open the locks in less than a minute. The three crowded around to look inside the valise. It was completely empty.

"Well, so much for diamonds," muttered Alice.

Jim ran his hand over the thin lining inside the box. There were no bulges or bumps. "It certainly doesn't seem like there is anything hidden in here."

They heard the sound of feet on the front porch, and Annie walked back out to meet Chief Edwards. He looked over the front room and shook his head. "I've sent some men over to Alice's house to check it out. We need to dust for fingerprints, but we'll try not to make a mess."

"Do what you need to do," Annie said. "I trust you. Oh, and I don't suppose one of your men could get Boots out of the tree before you leave?"

Chief Edwards grinned. "Sure, we try to be a full-service police department. Let's give her a few minutes to calm down, though. She might just waltz in here on her own."

Annie realized she should call Ian about the break-ins too. He would be upset if she didn't let him know. She called, trying to talk him out of racing right over, but she wasn't successful.

When Ian arrived, he took one look at the mess and turned to Annie. "That's it," he said. "I think both of you ladies should get rooms at Maplehurst Inn until whoever did this is arrested. I can hire someone to come in and put everything back in order."

Annie frowned. "I appreciate your take-charge attitude, Mr. Mayor, but I believe I can clean up my own house. I don't need more strangers poking around in my things."

"You're too vulnerable here," Ian insisted, stepping closer to her so that he seemed to tower over her. "I can't always be here to keep you safe."

Annie felt her temper rising. She didn't like feeling bullied, and definitely not by someone she considered a friend. "I called you because I didn't want you to be angry about not being told. I don't expect you to look after me, Ian Butler."

"Someone should," Ian snapped.

"Whoa!" Jim stepped up, holding up his hands as if separating two boxers. He gave Annie a sly wink. "Maybe we all need a moment to calm down."

Ian turned to face the craggy photographer, and Annie watched the two tall men try to stare each other down.

Alice caught Annie's glance and rolled her eyes, and then she stepped up. "How about we try a compromise?" Alice asked. "After the chief is done, we can spend a few hours helping Annie clean up and then get to the hotel before dark. I can call Linda and make sure she has a room. Would that work for you guys?"

"We don't need to be in a hotel. We can stay in your house," Jim said. "I'll be there. You don't have to worry."

Alice smiled. "But then Annie would be stuck in the hotel with those movie people, and we still don't know if one of them is a kidnapper."

Annie held up her hands. "I don't mind being at the inn, especially if Alice is with me. But I'm not leaving here with my house looking like this, and I want to be sure Boots is safe and sound inside."

Ian's nodded in agreement. Alice stepped into the relative quiet of the kitchen and made the call to the inn. When she came back, she smiled. "Linda even offered a special dispensation to Boots! She can stay in the room with us. Then it'll be as much like home as we can make it."

"As long as it doesn't last too long," Annie said. "I really am ready to be done with this mystery." Almost simultaneously with her last words, the phone in her pocket rang. Annie fished it out with shaking hands and saw only "Unknown Caller" on the caller ID screen.

"Hello?" she said softly.

"You're starting to make me angry." The raspy whisper made the back of Annie's neck tingle.

"That's not my intention. Look, we gave you the valise! What do you want?"

"I'm not stupid, lady," the man snarled. "That was the wrong bag. That means there must be a right bag, and you better start handing it over. So far, I haven't hurt anyone, but I'm starting to get annoyed."

Ian knew from Annie's pale face whose voice was on the other end of the line. He slipped back into the front room and got the chief. The chief snapped out his own phone and made a rolling motion with his finger. He wanted Annie to keep the man on the line.

"Maybe if you told me what you expected to find in the bag," Annie said, "we could make sure we bring what you actually want."

"Don't worry about that! Just worry about what I'm going to do to you if you don't hand over the goods! You're a pretty lady. Don't you want to stay that way?"

~ 16 ~

nnie felt her heart pounding in her chest. "There is another valise," she said, "and you're welcome to it."

"No tricks this time," he snarled. "And no cops. Don't make me sorry I let the redhead go without some damage."

Annie thought for a moment about what Alice had said to her and snapped, "I heard you were the one who was damaged that time."

"But not this time," he said. "You're going to bring me the bag today!"

The chief shook his head at Annie and began scribbling on a sheet of paper.

"I can't get to the bag today," Annie said. "I know where it is, but I won't be able to bring it to you today."

"I said no tricks," the raspy whisper changed to a shout, and for a second, Annie had that nagging feeling of familiarity again. She knew this voice. Where did she know it from? Was this someone she knew?

The chief handed her a piece of paper that read: "Tell him you'll do the handoff on Monday during the filming on the Town Square. It'll be easier to hide officers in the crowd of extras."

Annie nodded. "I can have the valise in the morning, but I'm not going anywhere alone with you. I don't want to end up tied up somewhere or worse. We can do the handoff at the movie set. I'm as eager to get rid of this thing as you are to get it."

"OK, bring it," the voice had dropped to a whisper again. "I'll find you when I'm sure you aren't setting me up."

The call dropped then. Annie looked up at the chief. "Was I on long enough?"

"We'll find out in a minute." The chief stepped out of the room, flipping open his cellphone.

Annie felt herself begin to shake, and she didn't resist when Ian stepped closer and put an arm around her. She looked up at Alice and asked, "Has that offer to spend the night with me at the inn expired?"

"Not a bit," Alice said. "Then tomorrow, we'll get this whole mess settled."

The chief looked grim as he rejoined them. "The cellphone the crook is using apparently has no GPS, or he has disabled it. He wasn't on long enough for us to triangulate and trace the call." He pointed at the valise on the table. "Is that what he's after?"

"I don't know," Annie said. "It doesn't make any sense. This bag is as empty as mine was."

The chief walked over and looked at the bag, snapping it open and running his hands over the lining just as Jim had. "Certainly seems empty."

Suddenly a horrible yowling screech made the whole group turn sharply toward the front door. A panicky-looking young officer came through the door carrying Boots, who was clearly trying to scrape away as much of the young man's skin as possible.

"Oh dear," Annie said, hurrying down the short hall toward the door.

The officer closed the door behind him with his foot and looked at Annie. "Can I put it down now?"

"Yes ... yes, you'd better."

The officer held Boots at arms length to keep the cat away from his face as he bent over. Then he dropped her lightly on the floor. Boots rocketed across the front room and up the stairs, nearly tripping another officer coming down when she rushed between his legs.

Annie rushed over to the young officer. "Oh, I'm so sorry. Did Boots scratch you?"

"Not too bad." The man's brown eyes were as warm as his smile. "My sister has an insane cat, and I've learned a lot about how to keep it away from my delicate areas. Still, I hope this one stays out of the tree."

"She normally does," Annie said. "We're all a little weirded out."

The man nodded. "I'm sure we'll be done soon. Do you need anything else?"

Annie shook her head, and then looked up. "Do you think the chief would mind if I started picking up in the rooms y'all have searched already?"

"I'll ask."

The officer strode across the room and leaned in close to speak quietly to the chief. Then he looked up and smiled at Annie as he crossed the room again. "The chief says we're done upstairs, and we should be done down here soon."

"Thank you." Annie went to the kitchen to tell everyone she was headed upstairs to start picking up.

"I'll come help," Alice said.

Annie shook her head. "You will have enough to do at your place, I'm sure."

Alice looked around the kitchen. "The guy did a more thorough job here. At my house I basically just have to shut drawers and kick stuff back into the closets." She smiled ruefully. "I never have had your way with organizing them."

At that, Annie remembered when she and Alice were just girls. Once, Annie had opened Alice's bedroom closet door to get a sweater and an avalanche of clothes, blankets, and sports equipment had rained down on her head. "You don't still use the pile and slam method?" she asked.

Alice shrugged. "Only in emergencies. At any rate, that means I can help you. To the upstairs!"

Ian insisted on helping too, though Annie sent him to the guest room. She didn't want Ian seeing the overturned dresser drawers in her own room. She appreciated Ian's generous help, but not enough to have him see a display of her underwear on the floor. Jim followed Ian, both men clearly having declared a truce of sorts to get through the job.

Alice began sorting the contents of Annie's bedroom floor onto the bed, so Annie could direct her to where each pile should end up. Annie turned to the closet, quickly returning crochet afghans and embroidered linens to storage bins to go back on top of the closet shelf.

Annie sighed as she pushed the last box onto the shelf and began picking up blouses and slacks to slip them back on the closet hangers. "I'm getting really tired of putting my house back together," she said. "Do you know, I think normal people might go through their whole lives without ever having their houses searched by strangers."

"True," Alice said, looking at her with a grin. "But what fun would it be if we had a normal life?"

Annie laughed. "I'm willing to risk the boredom. At least for a month or two."

"No you're not. If you were, you wouldn't have stayed in Stony Point. It's not like mysteries don't rain down on you constantly here. You're like a mystery lightning rod."

Annie looked concerned. "And all my friends risk the fallout. I'm so sorry for what that man put you through."

"Are you kidding?" Alice said. "Wait until we tell everyone on Tuesday. I'm a heroine!"

Annie laughed. Alice had always been good at turning wild escapades into grand adventures. She felt her mood lift considerably as they worked together. Then they heard a yell from the guest room.

Annie ran in to find Ian sitting on the guest room bed laughing until tears ran down his face as Jim glared at him. Boots sat in Ian's lap, eyeing Jim closely.

"What happened?" Annie asked.

"Your cat was hiding in the top of the closet," Jim said. "The thing jumped out and startled me."

"Startled?" Ian gasped. "Boots landed on his head like a clawed toupee, and then ran down his back while Jim swung at her with his cane and clunked himself in the forehead.

"You tried to hit Annie's cat?" Alice said, fighting her own laughter. "Shame on you!"

"It was trying to kill me," Jim protested.

"I'm sorry about that," Annie said. "I think I better put Boots in her carrier until we leave. She's had more than enough adventure for a while. Can you hold her for another minute?"

Ian stroked the chubby cat. "Sure, she seems happy."

"Yeah," Jim muttered. "She likes him."

Annie hurried back to her room for the carrier, and then slipped Boots in it. The cat gave her a dirty look and a crabby meow, but clearly she'd had enough excitement as well.

The rest of the cleaning went quicker than Annie expected. They were soon done upstairs and came downstairs just as Chief Edwards's team was packing up.

"You're going to be at Maplehurst?" the chief asked.

"Yes," Annie said. "Tonight."

"I'll call you to discuss the drop off of the valise tomorrow," the chief said. "Call me if anything unusual happens before then."

"I will," Annie assured him.

As soon as the police left, the rest of them worked on straightening up downstairs. Except for the kitchen, most of the mess was fairly quick and easy to handle. The burglar hadn't been destructive, just messy. Only in the kitchen did she see any sign of real temper—after all, she could hardly have been hiding the valise in her rice canister that he'd dumped on the floor.

Still, with a quick vacuuming, even that mess wasn't overly difficult. As she neared the end of the cleanup, Alice said, "I'm going next door to pack an overnight bag."

"Are you sure you want to stay with me?" Annie said. "Really, now that I've had some time to calm down, I'm sure I'll be fine."

"With that demon cat, I expect you could withstand an army," Jim said rubbing at a scratch on the back of his neck.

"Even so," Alice said. "I'm coming." She linked an arm through Jim's. "But you need to come next door with me so I can show you the mysteries of my furnace. It can be a little temperamental."

Annie smiled as Alice and Jim left, still arm in arm.

"He seems to make her happy," Ian said after they had gone.

"You seem surprised."

"I guess I didn't imagine Alice with someone so …"

"Romantic? Swashbuckling? Adventurous?"

"No—more like annoying."

Annie laughed. "I think he's sweet and fun."

Ian looked at her. "I can be fun."

"I know," she said. "We did karaoke."

"And a masquerade ball," he reminded her. "And a whale watch."

"You're the king of fun," she said, "and I'm done cleaning up. I'm going to run upstairs and pack my own overnight bag. You don't have to hang around here if you don't want to."

"I'm not letting you out of my sight until you're safe and sound in your room at the inn."

"The king of fun," Annie said as she walked out of the kitchen. "And the prince of bossy," she added over her shoulder.

Ian's warm laugh followed her up the stairs.

~ 17 ~

Annie's and Alice's room at Maplehurst Inn was surprisingly spacious for an old home-turned-inn. Annie suspected some major remodeling must have been done to turn the traditional New England closet-sized bedroom into the lovely open space in which she now stood.

The wall behind the headboards of the two beds was red brick. The headboards were a creamy vanilla, which went well with the hand-quilted vanilla and rose coverlet. Floral dust ruffles in the same shades added to the feminine look of the room.

"Very girlie," Annie said as she set Boots's carrier on the thick Oriental rug and opened it. The cat poked her nose out slowly, sniffing the air. Then she stepped daintily into the room.

Annie set up a small litter box in the bathroom near the lovely claw-foot tub. Then she put a small bowl of water and another half-filled with dry cat food in the bathroom as well. "That takes care of her highness," Annie said as she walked back into the bedroom area to find Boots curled up on the thickly cushioned window seat.

"She found the closest spot to the heat register," Alice said. "Smart kitty."

Annie took her clothes out of the small overnight bag and slipped them into one of the paper-lined drawers of the big dresser. Then she set her bag in the closet beside the empty valise. "This whole thing with the valise makes no sense," she said. "Why would someone want an empty valise this badly?"

"Maybe he doesn't," Alice said. "Maybe there's another valise with something valuable in it."

"Like still in with the other props?"

Alice shrugged. "Maybe. The guy got the bag we found in your attic, and it clearly wasn't what he wanted. And there is nothing in this one. It makes sense that there must be a third."

"Doesn't that seem like an awfully big coincidence?" Annie said. "Three identical bags in one spot? This would have to be the most common suitcase made."

"Still, maybe we should ask that prop guy."

Annie thought about it. "I know what room he's in. We could go see if he's there."

"Great." Alice stopped and stroked Boots fur. "If any bad guys come, attack!"

"Poor Boots," Annie said, rubbing the cat's ears until she purred. "I think she's had about all the strangers she can handle for one day."

Annie and Alice slipped out into the hall, carefully locking the room door behind them. They walked down the long hall and around the corner, passing several closed doors until Annie stopped in front of Samuel Ely's door and knocked. No one answered.

"Maybe he's downstairs," Alice said. "The weather is getting nasty out there, I can't imagine he's out touring the town."

Annie had to agree with her. That made sense. "Let's check downstairs."

The space in front of the lobby fireplace was filled with movie people again and Annie spotted the wardrobe and makeup people she'd met already, along with several casually dressed women she didn't know. "He's not at the fireplace."

"We could check in the dining room." Alice said. "And if some lunch tumbled into my mouth, I probably wouldn't resist too much."

Annie looked down at her watch and gasped. How had it gotten to be late afternoon so fast? "I'm sorry, Alice," she said. "I've been so nervous, I guess I haven't gotten hungry. We should eat."

Annie looked around the dining room as they walked in. Since it was late afternoon, only a scattering of people sat at the small tables, and none of them were the young prop master. At the far end of the room, double French doors opened into a bar area. A tall, thin girl stepped up to them quickly. "Two for lunch?"

"Yes, thank you," Annie said. "May we sit near that far end?"

"Of course." She led them to their table, filled their water glasses from a slightly damp metal pitcher, and handed them menus before slipping away.

"Why back here?"

"So I could look into the bar to see if Samuel was in there," Annie said.

"Is he?"

Annie leaned slightly back in her seat and looked into

the room. She saw several men from the film, including
Matt Rusher, but didn't see Samuel. "Nope." Before she
could lean forward again, she caught the actor's eye, and he
slipped off his stool and walked toward them.

"Oh dear," Annie muttered.

"What?" Alice said.

"What a nice surprise," Matt Rusher said as he stepped
out of the bar and stopped at their table. "I know I've met
you two lovely ladies before."

"It's nice to see you again, Mr. Rusher," Annie said,
folding her hands in her lap to avoid shaking his hand.

"Matt, please," he said. Then he turned to Alice who
hadn't gotten her hands out of sight quickly enough. He
lifted one of her hands to his mouth to kiss it. Annie noticed
he was wearing black leather gloves, which seemed odd in
the warm room.

Annie saw Alice smile thinly as she pulled her hand
away. "The weather's getting rough," she said. "I hope you
can film tomorrow."

"Well, it will save the cost of a snow machine," Matt
said. "I'm going to be standing in the falling snow, making
an impassioned plea to a hard-hearted town."

"Doesn't sound much like Stony Point," Annie said.

"You never know," Matt said. "Do you ladies mind if I
join you?"

"We were actually having a private conversation,"
Alice answered.

"Then I won't stay long," he said as he pulled over a
chair from a nearby table and pulled it up beside theirs. He
folded his arms over the back of the chair.

"Don't you get warm wearing gloves indoors?" Annie asked.

"I wear them all the time," Matt said. "It's my trademark. Haven't you seen my movies?"

"Yes, but it didn't occur to me that it would spill over into real life."

"After enough years in the business, real life and movie life blur," he said.

"I expect they would cover up age spots too," Alice said innocently as she took a sip from her water glass.

He looked at her and his charming smile turned cold. "I certainly don't have that problem."

"Certainly not."

The actor turned toward Annie, swiveling in his seat slightly to turn his shoulder toward Alice. Alice grinned over Matt's shoulder. "Are you going to be in tomorrow's shoot?"

"We both will," Alice said to Matt's shoulder. He chose not to answer her.

"Have you seen Samuel Ely today?" Annie asked.

"Who's that?"

"He works on the film," Alice said, still speaking to the actor's shoulder.

"I don't know everyone who works on the film," the man said. "There are so many of them, and they change constantly. You wouldn't believe how many people scurry around behind the scenes."

"You make them sound like mice," Annie said.

"Or roaches." Alice was clearly enjoying injecting comments and watching the actor try to turn more and more of his back to her. Annie could hear the laughter in Alice's voice.

"They have their jobs," the actor said with a shrug, "and I have mine."

"This is a very different film for you, isn't it?" Annie asked.

"My agent thought it would be good for me to do a film for the ladies."

At that Alice laughed out loud, and the actor stood with a grumble. "I have to go," he said, still speaking only to Annie. "I hope to see you tomorrow on set."

"Maybe," Annie said.

The actor stalked out of the room, and Alice laughed even harder.

"You're incorrigible," Annie said.

"Oh, it's good for him," Alice said. "He acts like he's started to believe his own press. That can't be good for the guy."

Alice was still chuckling when the waitress came up to their table. "Sorry to make you wait," she said, dropping her voice. "That actor can be a little ... inappropriate." Then she looked worried. "I'm sorry. I shouldn't have said that. Is he a friend of yours?"

"He certainly isn't a friend of mine," Alice said, her voice still a bit giggly.

"Don't worry about it," Annie said. "I'm sure Mr. Rusher can be challenging to serve. Have things been busy here the last few days?"

The girl nodded. "I was expecting to be laid off. I don't blame Linda, of course. There just isn't usually much business this time of year. But the film company has made us have all hands on deck here."

"I'm glad to see it's doing the town some good," Annie said as she glanced down at her menu. "I'd like the lobster bisque please."

Alice ordered a cup of the same soup, but added a thick sandwich to go with it. "I am starving," she admitted.

"It should be out quickly," the waitress assured them. "The crowd has finally thinned down. If you'd been here more at lunchtime, you might have had to wait a while." Then she sighed. "Not that the movie people like to wait."

The girl turned and hurried away to put in their order.

"She'd best make sure Linda doesn't hear her complaining about the customers," Alice said. "She'd get an earful then."

"You're not going to tell on her."

Alice held up her hands. "Not me," she said. "I've had enough times in my life when someone could have told on me."

They chatted then for a bit about escapades from when they were kids. Soon Alice had Annie laughing, and by the time the food came she finally felt like she could eat it. The bisque smelled lovely and tasted buttery and smooth. She moaned softly.

"Maplehurst makes the best lobster bisque I've ever had," Alice said. "Never tell my mother I said that."

That made Annie laugh. "I remember having corn chowder at your house as a kid. It was basically milky canned corn with bacon bits sprinkled in it."

"Mom didn't even use real bacon bits. She used those horrible crunchy things that you're supposed to put on salad." Alice shook her head. "I'm telling you, sneaking away to eat at Betsy's house is the only thing that kept me alive as a kid.

"Gram was a fantastic cook," Annie said. "But I think you've surpassed her when it comes to baking."

Alice looked surprised. "Well, thank you. I take that as the highest possible compliment."

When the waitress came to bring them their check and pick up the dishes, Annie asked her if she knew where Samuel Ely might be. "He's tall and thin with glasses and a bit of a beard," she said.

The waitress's face pinked up. "I know Samuel," she said. "I believe he's in the library."

"The inn has a library?" Annie said.

"Well, it's a room with books," Alice said. "I know where it is."

"It's really nice and cozy with its own fireplace," the waitress said. "Samuel likes to go there."

After the girl hurried away to get their change, Annie whispered to Alice. "I get the feeling she isn't tired of all the movie people."

"Yeah, it looks like your prop-master friend has a fan."

"He seems like a really nice guy," Annie said. "Well, let's go visit the library."

Alice led her easily through the slight maze of rooms on the first floor. Since the inn had been remodeled to make a large lobby and the big dining room space, some of the other rooms had shrunk and the hallways were narrow.

When they made what seemed like their tenth turn, Annie said, "Apparently this library is only for really committed readers."

"It used to be in a bigger room," Alice said. "But apparently it didn't get much use. Here we are."

The room was about the size of Annie's living room at Grey Gables with a tiny fireplace at one end. All of the other walls were covered with custom bookshelves from floor to ceiling. Two leather chairs and a leather love seat were grouped around a coffee table at the center of the room. Annie saw Samuel in one of the two chairs.

The young man looked up at them, surprise shining in his eyes. He pushed his glasses up on his nose with one finger. "Mrs. Dawson," he said.

"Hello, Samuel. We're sorry to disturb you," she said. "This is my friend Alice McFarlane. I wanted to ask you something about the valise."

"Oh, right. You thought you'd need the receipt," he said. "I have it here." He stood so he could pull his wallet out of the back pocket of his jeans. Then he slipped the receipt out of the wallet. "See, I bought three cases at this thrift shop near Boston. This one is the one you borrowed. It was twenty bucks."

"I will need to pay for it, but I actually have another question. Did you happen to buy any other suitcases that looked like that one?"

"You mean just like it?" he asked, and she nodded. He paused to consider it and finally said. "I had a couple that looked a little like it. You saw one of them—same leather sides, but it had gold metal trim. And there was one that was black, but it had the leather trim and silver caps. So not the same."

Annie nodded. She'd known it was a long shot. "Thanks

Samuel. Here, let me give you the money for the case." She
pulled her wallet out of her small purse and paid him. "By the
way, we met a waitress here who seems to think well of you."

"Ally?" Samuel said as his face grew red under his
scruffy beard.

"We didn't catch her name," Alice said. "But she knew
right where to find you."

"Must be Ally. I met her in here. She likes to read on
her breaks." He sighed then. "She doesn't like my smoking."

"One more good reason to quit then," Annie said.

Samuel smiled a little. "I guess. Did she really seem to
like me?"

"Looked that way to us," Alice replied.

Samuel pushed his glasses up on his nose and rubbed
the back of his neck. "Thanks for telling me. Maybe you're
right, Mrs. Dawson. It just might be time to quit."

"Good luck," Annie said.

Then she and Alice turned toward the door to leave
Samuel with his own thoughts. At the last moment, Annie
turned back. "Has anyone shown any unusual interest in
the props for this film?"

Samuel laughed. "You mean anyone besides you?"

"Right."

Samuel gave it a moment of thought. "No, really it's
been a pretty normal shoot—chaotic, crazy and everyone
changing things on me at the last minute. For a movie,
that's about as normal as it gets."

"Thanks, Samuel," she said, and both women left
the room.

"And you scold the rest of us for being matchmakers,"

Alice said as soon as they'd gone a ways down the hall. "I'm telling on you to the Hook and Needle Club."

"Like the Hook and Needle Club needs any encouragement." Then Annie sighed. "Well, there went our last lead. I guess we can just go up to the room and stare at each other."

Alice laughed. "You certainly make that seem appealing. Let's sit by the fire in the lobby instead. You never know what we might pick up."

"Eavesdropping?" Annie asked.

"People watching ... ," Alice answered, "... and maybe some eavesdropping."

The group around the fireplace in the lobby had grown smaller, but Annie spotted Betty and Pat still there, their heads leaning slightly toward one another as they argued cheerfully about something.

Annie settled into a velvet-covered wing chair close to the fire. The fire snapped and crackled beside her. She watched the flames squirm and dance as the logs slowly turned to coals. In one, the fire seemed to have burrowed into the wood, making red light that looked like dozens of tiny eyes peering out from deep in the log.

"You must really like this inn!"

Betty's sharp voice made Annie jump and she looked at the older woman, only to find Betty was looking straight at her. "Oh, me?" Annie said. "Actually I'm having a problem at my house, so I'm staying here tonight."

"A problem?" Betty's eyes sparkled with curiosity. "A gas leak? A raccoon in the attic? Or you forgot to get your chimney swept and lit a fire, and now the whole house is full of smoke!"

"Oh, Betty," Pat scolded. "What an imagination you have."

"It wasn't any of those things," Annie said. "Are you both enjoying the break in filming?"

Betty harrumphed. "We didn't get a break. The company filmed a touching scene between that nice boy Logan and his cranky father yesterday. Well, at least they tried to. That Matt Rusher has turned out to be harder to corral than a cat."

"Really?" Alice said, and the older lady's eyes turned to her sharply.

"Betty," Pat said firmly, "we shouldn't be talking about the talent."

Betty harrumphed again. "So they can fire me," she said. "This may be a movie, but the pay isn't that wonderful. My cousin gets more for painting makeup on dead people for a funeral home in Florida."

"Betty!" Pat gasped.

"It's true. My cousin trowels more makeup on those poor dead folks than Vernee there."

A bright cackle of laughter made Annie turn to see the woman who did such an amazing job of swooping her hair into a smooth twist for the movie. "You do hair and makeup?" Annie asked.

"Magic hands," Vernee said, holding up her long-fingered hands. "But as for your cousin, Betty, she deserves the money for handling dead folks, in my opinion."

"Sure, but it seems like a nice retirement job," Betty said. "They don't wiggle or complain. And they don't mess up their wardrobe." She cut her eyes toward Annie.

Annie felt a faint blush creep over her face.

"Now, don't go teasing the girl," Pat said. "She already

apologized about the stockings."

Annie smiled a little. It wasn't often she was called a "girl" anymore. "I'm sure it can be trying," she said, "working with so many people and so many different personalities."

"Mostly celebrities are just like anyone else," Pat said. "They have good days and bad days. Some are just sweethearts, like that Lariby boy. And some tend to wear their bad mood right out where you can see it. That can happen with anyone." This time Pat gave a meaningful look at Betty.

"Are you calling me bad tempered?" Betty asked.

"If the grouch fits … ."

Alice burst into laughter at the two women. They were so clearly old friends that anyone could tell that none of the squabbling was real. "So, have you ladies seen anything weird since you got to Stony Point?" Alice asked.

"The weather's pretty strange," Vernee said. "One day it's cold enough to freeze flame, and the next everything's dripping. How do you get used to it?"

"I'm still working on it," Annie said, "but I think Alice was wondering if anyone has been behaving oddly."

The older women looked at each other, and then burst into peals of laughter. It took several minutes for them to calm down. "I'm sorry, dear," Pat said when she caught her breath. "I don't mean to laugh at you, but we work in Hollywood. There really isn't anything we would consider odd behavior anymore."

"I once knew an actor who absolutely would not go on set unless he was wearing blue boxer shorts," Betty said. "I had the worst time with wardrobe for that man. But he was sure that if he wore anything but blue boxer shorts, his career would tank."

"What happened to him?" Alice asked.

Betty grinned at her mischievously. "His career tanked."

Again the women laughed, though this time Annie and Alice were caught up in it as well.

Finally, the laughter calmed again and Pat looked closely at Alice. "Exactly what kind of weird thing are you interested in?"

"I really don't know," Alice admitted. "But we've had a very strange past few days."

"Well of course you have," Vernee said. "Hollywood has come to town. We'd be disappointed if that didn't mean weird things for you."

The other women nodded. Alice and Annie exchanged a glance. No help with the mystery here. Then they both smiled and settled back comfortably in their chairs.

"OK, so tell me," Alice said. "What other stories of Hollywood weirdness do you have?"

"Oh, honey," Pat said. "Actors are crazy—just crazy. We used to have this beautiful wood cabinet that we carried all our gloves and scarves in. But the actors absolutely couldn't pass that thing without knocking on the wood. It was like living next to a giant woodpecker all day long."

"I was ready to burn that thing," Betty grumbled.

"We finally had poor Samuel haul it off for us when we were working on *Aliens in the Afterlife*," Pat said. "I think he sold it at one of those thrift stores he's so fond of."

"So you've worked with Samuel before?" Annie asked.

"Hollywood is a smaller world than you think," Vernee chimed in. "We cross paths constantly."

"He seems like a nice young man," Annie said.

"He's a sweetheart," Pat said, and the other two women nodded.

Alice and Annie passed another hour or so listening to star stories from the three women. Annie was almost glad she'd had to move to Maplehurst Inn for the night; she would never have gotten to spend this much time with these spirited women otherwise.

Finally though, Pat caught Betty nodding off twice and the group broke up to head on to bed. "Well, that wasn't really productive," Alice said as they climbed the winding staircase to the second-floor rooms, "but it sure was fun."

Annie nodded. "I haven't laughed so much in a while."

As they stood outside the room, Annie felt a small twinge of nerves. She was actually a little afraid to go into her room. They'd had so many unpleasant surprises lately. She looked at Alice.

"Yeah," Alice said. "Closed doors can hide so much. Time to be brave." She thrust her key in the lock and turned it. The door swung open to show the pleasant room exactly as they'd left it. Boots looked up from her warm spot on the window seat and blinked at them.

"Now I just feel silly," Annie said.

"After the last few days, I think we totally have a right to be silly."

They bustled around for a bit, slipping into cozy pajamas. Then the same thought hit them again. "I'm not really sleepy yet," Annie said.

"Want to watch a movie?" Alice asked. She glanced at the clock on the table between the beds. "*Titanic* is on in five minutes. I love that movie."

"Oh, that would be perfect. Too bad we don't have popcorn."

"Who says we don't?" Alice walked to the closet and picked up her bag. She pulled out an unopened bag of popcorn. "It's not quite like fresh made, but it's close."

"Absolutely perfect," Annie replied.

Alice poured half the bag of popcorn into the ice bucket and kept the other half for herself. Then they each climbed into bed, pulling the fluffy comforters over their laps and settled in to watch the movie. Soon, Boots gave up her window seat to settle down beside Annie and eat the occasional piece of dropped popcorn.

Annie made it to the end of the popcorn, but after that, she sunk lower and lower in the bed until she nodded off. She dreamt of riding at the prow of a ship with Wayne as the wind blew her hair. Nothing dark or scary crept into the dream in the night, and she woke with a smile still on her lips.

~18~

When Annie woke, Alice was already up and carrying Boots around, cooing to the cat. "You shouldn't do that," Annie said. "Boots is already totally full of herself."

Alice smiled. "She's a princess, and she knows it. I called home, and Jim said that film crew called after we left yesterday. We need to be at the library in two hours. Apparently the crew took over their meeting-room spaces to use for wardrobe and such."

Annie swung her feet over the side of her bed. "Somehow I didn't picture Jim as an early riser."

"He's not," Alice said laughing. "And he has a colorful vocabulary if you wake him up by letting the phone ring until he gives up and answers it."

"That, I can believe." Annie headed into the spacious bathroom for a quick shower. As she passed the counter, she accidentally nudged the small cat bowl with the toe of her slipper. At the scraping sound, Boots rushed into the bathroom and peered into the bowl. Then she glanced up at Annie. "Sorry—accident."

The cat turned and stalked back out of the room.

Annie finished her preparations as quickly as possible. "I might be a little late to the shoot," she said. "I need to take Boots home first so we can check out."

"Let me make a call," Alice said. She called down to the

front desk and had a short chat with Linda Hunter. Finally she smiled and shoved the phone into her pocket. "Linda said not to worry about anything. We can come pick up the stuff after filming today. Hopefully, the whole mystery will be over by then, and you can feel safe taking Boots home."

"That's nice of Linda," Annie said.

"Linda is great," Alice said, "but I think she also hopes I'll make another big batch of muffins and coffee cake tonight. So she's being especially agreeable."

"Well, your muffins always make me feel very agreeable," Annie said.

The soft thump of Boots jumping back up on the window seat drew their attention. Alice walked over and pulled open the window curtains. "Look, it's snowing pretty hard," she said. "That makes me glad I'm not driving to the shoot."

"I think I'll have a nice bowl of oatmeal with fruit and nuts for breakfast," Annie said. "Maybe it'll help me stay warm out there."

"Good plan," Alice said.

They headed down to the breakfast room and found the oatmeal hot and creamy, and exactly what they wanted on such a snowy day. The breakfast room was bustling with people. Most were finishing up as Annie and Alice walked in.

Annie looked around the room. Even in a casual setting like breakfast, all of the younger members of the crew looked so intense and purposeful. Most of the older people, like the ladies Annie and Alice had so enjoyed chatting with the night before, seemed more relaxed. Annie guessed they'd already climbed the ladder of success to wherever they cared to be and didn't feel the need for the same fretful intensity. Still, it was interesting to watch.

By the time Annie and Alice paid their bill, the room had emptied out. "Now I feel like we're going to be fashionably late," Annie said.

"Not by my watch," Alice answered. "Remember, we're just extras. All the real movie people have to be there before us."

Annie nodded, but it was still disconcerting to be alone in the room after all the energy that had filled the space so recently. Annie and Alice slipped into their coats, scarves, hats, and gloves to prepare for the cold, snowy weather waiting for them.

"I need to run up and get the valise," Annie said. "I didn't want to bring it down to breakfast."

"I'll wait by the door."

Annie hurried upstairs and gave Boots a quick pat for luck or comfort. Then she grabbed the valise and hoped the drop would work out this time. Alice's kidnapping had scared the curiosity right out of her. Now all she wanted was for it to be over.

Annie felt a flood of relief when she saw Alice still standing safely by the front door. When they walked out into the snow, Annie blinked at the icy flakes that floated down to lay on her lashes. "At least it's not windy," she said.

"Right. It wouldn't be very picturesque to film one of our blizzards where it snows sideways," Alice said as she stepped carefully down the front steps of the inn. The snow was thin on the steps, and it showed signs of someone having been out to clear them—probably several times already.

The sidewalk had more snow compacted by the feet that

had gone before. Annie clutched the valise carefully and watched her feet. The snow allowed visibility only a short way ahead, so it was actually just about as clear to simply stare down at the sidewalk. Since they needed to walk straight ahead for a little over a block, all she had to do was avoid wandering out into the street, or veering left and stumbling into one of the storefronts.

"I feel like I stepped into *Little House on the Prairie*," Alice said. "Should we tie ourselves together?"

Annie laughed and reached out to take Alice's arm. "We could hold onto each other," she said. "I don't see how they can film in this though."

"Maybe they're hoping it'll lighten up a little," Alice said. "Oh, who's that?"

Annie looked up and spotted the still figure Alice must have meant. With the snowflakes stinging her eyes, it was difficult for her to tell who the person might be. Who would just stand around outside in this?

They pressed on and Annie was amazed at how long the block seemed to have grown. They passed the movie theater and A Stitch in Time. By then, the shadowy figure had become clearer.

"Good morning, ladies," Jim Parker said as he stood leaning on his cane not far from the door of The Cup & Saucer.

"What are you doing out here in the snow?" Alice asked. "Are you trying to catch pneumonia?"

Jim laughed, a rumbling sound from deep in his chest. "Sweetheart, it'll take a lot more than a little snow to kill someone like me."

Alice just shook her head. "That still doesn't explain what you're doing out here."

"I couldn't wait another minute to see my best girl," he said, leaning close to give Alice a kiss on the cheek, "and her best friend." And he gave Annie a quick peck as well.

"Well, we have to head over to the library and get suited up for this filming," Alice said.

"I'll come with you," Jim said.

"I don't know if they'll let you be an extra since you didn't fill out the forms," Annie said.

"That's OK," he said. "I'm not really the actor type. But I plan to be nearby. The man who had the nerve to kidnap my girl is close, and I'd like to chat with him."

Annie was startled again by how fierce Jim could be. She suspected anyone who might think Jim an easy target because of his handicap would quickly learn differently.

They headed on to the library and Annie turned to Jim. "Could you hold this for me until I'm done in wardrobe?" she asked. "I don't want to draw too many questions about why I'm carrying it, since it's not part of this shoot."

"No problem," Jim said. "I feel better with it in my hands anyway. I'd love the guy to come try to get it early."

Annie patted his arm. "Don't go getting in any fights. Alice would never forgive me."

Jim just smiled. Annie and Alice were hustled off to the women's wardrobe department. Pat and Betty greeted them with the warm squabbling they'd come to associate with the two women.

"I don't envy you standing out in that blizzard this morning," Betty said as she pulled a wool suit out of a rack and handed it to Annie along with some thick stockings and sensible shoes. "We'll have a coat for you too, but put these on for now."

"This isn't a blizzard," Alice said. "It's a light snow."

Betty just rolled her eyes at Alice and rooted through the rack for another outfit.

Today, hair and makeup consisted of twisting their hair up with a few pins and cramming a hat over the result. "Today they won't be shooting your faces, really," Vernee told them. "Now just join the crowd in the library lobby. They'll shoo you outside when they're ready to film."

They walked back to the library lobby. With the wool suits and heavy coats and hats, they were a little too warm in the lobby, but Annie knew that would pass quickly once they got outside.

She looked around and spotted Jim, leaning on one of the big display cases. The women walked over to stand with him. Jim tapped the glass case. "These are gorgeous."

Annie looked through the glass. The case contained a variety of old postcards from across New England. To her, they mostly looked faded and bent. "Gorgeous?" she said.

"They're history," he said. "Look, you can see the backs of these. Look at those old stamps and the handwriting. No one writes like that anymore." He shook his head. "It's like seeing a little speck from someone's life. You would be surprised how much American history is built from old letters or postcards, just like these."

Annie nodded and looked closer at the cards. She squinted to read the cramped writing. The ones that were arranged to show the print were chosen specifically because they said interesting things. On one, a woman was gushing about how she had seen President Kennedy sailing. Another was a card from a woman who was writing from New York City, where she'd gone expecting to meet her sister's ship— the RMS Titanic.

"Oh," Annie said softly, "I see what you mean."

"What are we looking at?" A familiar male voice said from behind her, making Annie jump as she was pulled back from her musing on the past.

"This postcard is about the Titanic," Annie said, turning to smile at Ian. "A woman waiting on her sister. I wonder if her sister made it home safely."

"The Titanic?" Alice said. "Hey, we just watched that movie. And speaking of movies, do you think they're going to be able to film today?"

Ian nodded. "The snow is letting up. But they'll probably want to get this scene in as few takes as possible. I think they'll be sending us outside any time now."

Annie looked up at the mayor and smiled. "How come you're not wearing a hat."

Ian shrugged. "Maybe my haircut is old-fashioned enough to pass," he said, and then he smiled. "Or they ran out of hats."

His words were followed almost immediately by another voice calling for everyone's attention. Annie looked up to spot the thin, nervous assistant who clearly was in charge of riding herd over extras for every shoot. She felt badly about always thinking of him as "the nervous guy" and made a mental note to introduce herself to the man before the end of the day.

"Today you're playing an angry crowd," the young man shouted from near the library doors. "We don't want a lot of sound. That will be added in post-production. Instead, as you stand together, just move a lot. Don't move off your mark, just twist from side to side a little, roll your shoulders, look around a lot. Keep the movements sharp to look angry." The young man jerked his arms and shoulders, snapping his neck from side to side to show them the kind of movements he wanted. "You don't need to be in constant motion. We don't want you to look like you're having convulsions. Keep the movements small but sharp. OK, let's see you try it. Bunch up a little here."

He waved a hand to draw the crowd together. Annie, Alice and Ian stepped away from the display case with the rest. They practiced looking restless, and the young assistant coached them. Finally they must have looked good enough.

"Now we'll go out to the Town Square," the young man said. "You'll see a platform we've put up, stand at least fifteen feet back from that. I'll help you get in place once we get there. Be careful on the steps and in crossing the street. We've blocked off traffic, but the pavement is slippery. Ready?"

Annie stepped back over and took the case from Jim.

"Good luck," he said. "I'll be close by."

"Thanks."

She walked back over to stand by Ian and Alice. As she passed the young assistant on the way out the door, she took care to shield the valise with her body so he wouldn't see it and ask about why she'd be carrying it in this scene.

Outside, the snow fell in fat flakes that quickly piled up

on Annie's coat sleeves, but the visibility was much better. She could see the Town Square across the street and the platform the assistant had mentioned.

She followed the rest of the crowd across the street, but made sure to hang as close as possible to the edges of the crowd. She didn't want the kidnapper to have trouble finding her and collecting the valise.

Ian leaned close to her. "Chief Edwards doesn't like this idea much," he said. "With the snow and the huge number of people moving around, it's going to be hard to grab the guy once he goes for the valise. At least visibility has gotten better."

Annie nodded. She had held the handle of the valise with both hands, keeping it around to the front of her body until Ian took her arm to speak in her ear. She looked from side to side, remembering to keep her movements sharp and agitated like the assistant had asked. Luckily it also gave her a chance to watch for anyone approaching.

She heard someone yell from the edge of the crowd. "Action!"

Annie wondered if the man would dare go for the valise while the cameras were rolling. Wouldn't he run the risk of being caught on film? She kept looking sharply from side to side.

"More movement," a voice shouted. "Push a little. Don't knock anyone over."

The crowd moved restlessly around her, and it became harder to stay in the back. Annie felt a bump on her elbow and turned to look sharply. No one seemed to be looking at her, and she still held the valise tightly.

She reached up with her free hand to wipe at the snow collecting on her eyelashes. When she put her hand down again, she turned to look at Ian, but the person beside her was a tall woman in a black coat. The woman held up a fist and shook it. For a moment Annie worried about the woman's glaring anger, but then she remembered they were acting.

Annie looked around, trying to spot Ian's salt-and-pepper hair in the group around them. With most of the crowd wearing hats, Ian should be relatively easy to spot, she thought, but the crowd was so dense.

Annie took a calming breath. Ian would soon realize she wasn't beside him, and then he would come to her. Then she jumped when a voice boomed over the crowd. "CUT!"

"Oh good," Annie whispered. The crowd would stop pushing, and Ian would have an easier time getting back to her. She continued to scan the crowd as she waited.

Then her eyes widened in surprise. Logan Larriby slipped through the crowd and walked to her. "Hi, Mrs. Dawson," he said as he stopped next to her.

"Hello, Logan," Annie said. "Are you not in this scene?"

"I am, but I'm on a break," Logan said. "There's something wrong with the setup on the stage." He shrugged. "It looked fine to me, but I guess it wasn't."

Annie scouted around for something to say. "Did you have a nice weekend?"

He shrugged again. "We shot some scenes. Same old, same old. Do you know if Vanessa is back?"

Annie smiled. "I believe she is. In fact, she's probably in the crowd somewhere." She expected Logan to excuse himself then and go looking for her, instead he just stuffed his hands in his pockets and rocked back and forth on his heels.

Annie began to worry a bit. Would the kidnapper approach with the young actor beside her? Should she make him go away? Annie wasn't sure what to do, but she was desperate for this to work. How could she make the boy go away without ruining everything?

~19~

"Maybe you should work your way through the crowd at little," Annie said. "I bet you could find Vanessa." Logan nodded, but he didn't move away. He looked around though, as if he thought Vanessa might suddenly pop out of the crowd. Annie wondered if maybe he was playing it cool, not wanting to look desperate.

"She'll be happy to see you," she said encouragingly.

"She's great," he said. "She's smart and really funny. And she's not as into herself as a lot of the girls in California."

"She's a lovely girl." Annie began to fret that she was going to have to demand the boy go away.

Finally, Logan turned to face her. "OK, I better just take the suitcase then."

"What?" Annie stared at him in shock.

"The suitcase?" he said pointing at the valise. "You need to give me the suitcase!"

Annie's eyes darted over the crowd then as she meekly handed over the case. Did Chief Edwards have a man close by? Would they see that Logan had the case? She couldn't believe the nice young actor had been the hateful voice on the phone.

"Thanks," Logan said, flashing her a grin. "I'll hunt up Vanessa after the shoot. Thanks, Mrs. Dawson." He turned sharply and began to walk toward the street.

Since they were on something of a break, the crowd had
begun to spread out a little, and Annie watched the young
actor weave around people. She expected to see Ian or some
of the police officers step up to the actor, but no one did.
Maybe they had missed the whole thing.

Annie felt a flush of anger. That young man had scared
her half to death. He'd kidnapped Alice. He'd torn up her
house. How could he grin at her like it was all some kind of
game? Suddenly she absolutely refused to let him get away.
She started after him just as she heard a voice bellow from
the sidelines.

"OK, we're going to start again," the voice shouted.
"Everyone back in place, and let's really get angry this time."

The people who had drifted from the clump hurried back,
stepping in Annie's way as she continued to follow Logan.
Each time Annie brushed by someone, she was aware of their
annoyed glances. One man was in such a hurry to regroup
with the crowd of extras, he nearly knocked Annie down as
she reached the slippery sidewalk.

Once she was on the edge of the street, Annie was finally clear of the crowd. She looked around but couldn't
see Logan anywhere. She did see Alice off to her left racing
across the street.

"Alice must have seen Logan with the case," Annie muttered to herself as she stepped carefully out on the snowy
street. She wasn't as confident running in this weather as
Alice, but she couldn't bear the thought of leaving her friend
in danger again. Annie picked up her pace, gritting her teeth
as she hoped she wouldn't fall.

The blocked-off street had offered the snow a nice clear

surface to build upon. Already the fat flakes had layered to enough inches that they slipped over the edge of Annie's sensible shoes, and she felt the wet and cold numbing her feet.

Annie had nearly reached the other side of the street, and she considered yelling at Alice to get her to wait, but her friend angled toward the buildings and slipped into the narrow alley between the movie theater and A Stitch in Time.

Annie had barely been aware there was an alley there! The sidewalk was only slightly clearer than the street; the business owners had been out to clear away the snow. The thick flakes had only begun to spread a cover back over the concrete.

Annie reached the alley and peeked in. She saw Alice creeping through. The alley was so narrow that Alice had to walk slightly turned; stepping sideways had slowed her gait considerably. Annie slipped into the space.

Her own narrower shoulders required less sideways turn, and the walls of the two buildings had kept most of the snow out of the narrow gap. This meant Annie could walk faster than Alice through the alley. The ground at her feet was littered with debris blown in by the wind, mostly soft-drink cups and popcorn boxes from the theater next door. Still, the scuffling through the debris made Annie jump once or twice as bits of cardboard scraped past one of her ankles.

At least she was pretty sure it was too cold for rats to be creeping through the alley. Suddenly she was sorry she'd entertained any thought of rats because her imagination turned every scrape and rustle into a hairy rodent.

Finally she caught up to Alice and put a hand on her

friend's shoulder. Alice jumped and gasped. She jerked her head toward Annie, and then her whole body clearly relaxed one notch. "You almost scared me to death," Alice said, her voice barely above a breath.

"Sorry," Annie whispered back.

Alice took Annie's hand and together they half-walked, half-scooted the rest of the way down the alley. Finally the gloom of the narrow space gave way to the glare of snow on pavement.

They saw Logan Lariby standing with the valise in his hands, looking around the parking lot. "What's he waiting for?" Alice whispered back at Annie.

Annie shook her head. She had no idea.

Suddenly, another man stepped from around the end of a van. His bulky black peacoat, dark scarf and ski mask made him impossible to recognize. The young actor seemed surprised by the other man's clothes. He leaned toward the bulkier figure and spoke, but Annie couldn't make out what he said.

The bulky figure took the valise from Logan.

"That's it," Alice muttered. She stepped out into the bright light of the parking lot. "Hold it right there!"

The young actor turned and looked at Alice in surprise. Then he looked back at the bulky figure as if expecting the second man to explain. The second man didn't speak; he just backed away with the valise in his hand.

"Where do you think you're going?" Alice yelled again, striding toward them across the lot. Annie wasn't sure it was a good idea to confront a man who was a mugger, housebreaker and kidnapper, but she wasn't going to leave Alice on her own, so she strode forward with her friend.

"This is my property," the bulky figure growled, his voice muffled by the scarf and ski mask. "I'm taking it back."

"What's going on?" Logan asked. The confusion on his young face was almost comical.

"He's a thief and a kidnapper," Annie yelled, pointing at the other figure.

"I think you've made a mistake," Logan said, but just then the other man bolted and ran.

"Get him!" Alice yelled.

Logan looked first at the fleeing man, and then back at Annie, his eyes questioning.

"Yes, he's a bad guy," she said.

That seemed to be enough. The young actor turned sharply and dashed after the running man. With his youth and long-legged stride, he caught up easily and tackled the bulkier figure. Together they slammed onto the floor of the snowy parking lot.

Logan struggled to hold the other man down, but even though Logan was quick, the other man outweighed him by nearly fifty pounds, and Logan soon went flying. Annie saw the young actor's head smack the bumper of a nearby car with a dull thump.

The bigger man scrambled to his feet still clutching the valise. Alice ran after him, but Annie yelled, "Alice, we need to help Logan."

Alice looked between the young man on the ground and the running man and groaned. Annie didn't blame her. It looked like the kidnapper was going to get away again, but she couldn't just leave Logan on the ground.

The thief had reached the end of the short row of shops and was clearly angling toward the buildings to run back up Oak Lane toward Main Street. Then, just as he reached the edge of the building, another man stepped out into the open. The thief tried to jag around the newcomer, but the man simply strode a step closer and punched the thief in the face. Between the force of the punch and his own momentum, the thief was thrown hard to the ground. The valise flew from the thief's hand and slid under the closest parked car.

Alice gave a cry of joy and ran toward the hero of the moment. It was Jim Parker, rubbing his knuckles as he grinned at Alice. "That really felt good," Jim said as Alice threw her arms around his neck, "but not as good as this!"

Annie knelt beside Logan as the alley grew very busy, very fast. The young actor had a gash on his forehead that was leaking an alarming amount of blood. Annie used the soft white scarf they'd given her as part of her costume to staunch the flow of blood. *Betty and Pat are going to be annoyed with me again*, she thought as the blood soaked through the fabric.

Logan blinked at her. "What's going on?" he asked.

"Do you know who that is?" she asked, gesturing toward the sprawled figure in the snow. As she spoke, more men came around the corner, including Chief Edwards. They swarmed past Jim and toward the prone thief.

"Of course," Logan said.

More men came through the narrow alley, spilling into the parking lot. Annie recognized Ian as he came through the gap and rushed toward her. Annie looked down at

Logan. "Well, who is it?"

She looked toward the figure as Chief Edwards pulled the man's ski mask off and Logan Lariby said, "It's Mr. Rusher."

Annie stared at the scowling face of the actor as Chief Edwards read him his rights.

"Wow," Alice said with a grin. "Now there's a story. I was kidnapped by a movie star. The Hook and Needle Club is going to be blown away!"

Annie stood up, remembering something. "Alice, didn't you say you bit your kidnapper? That you were pretty sure you left a mark?"

"Oh right, I did." Alice walked toward the handcuffed actor. "I bit him on the right hand."

Chief Edwards leaned Matt Rusher forward with a sharp push and tugged off the man's right glove. His hand was deeply bruised and Annie could clearly see the pattern of Alice's bite.

"That's my girl!" Jim said.

Alice narrowed her eyes. "I didn't appreciate spending the day tied up and cold."

"Tough," the actor snarled.

"What could you possibly want with that old valise?" Annie asked. "Alice and I looked at it—at both of them. They're just old suitcases."

"I'm not saying anything without my lawyer," the actor said.

"That's probably a good idea, Mr. Rusher," Chief Edwards said as he hauled the man to his feet. Then the chief looked toward the young man who still sat in the snow with a scarf pressed to his head. "We've called the EMTs, but we'll want to speak with you too."

"That's fine," Logan said. "I'd like to know what's going on. I'm not in any trouble am I?"

"I doubt it," Annie said. "It looks like you were just being used to take the fall. What did Mr. Rusher tell you about the valise?"

"You should shut up, kid," Matt Rusher snapped. "Get a lawyer."

Logan blinked a few times. "I don't know why I would need one. Mr. Rusher told me he had loaned the valise to the props department, and you'd accidentally taken it home. He said you had it at the shoot so you could return it. He said he needed to talk to the director about the shoot and asked me to get it during the break." He turned and frowned. "He said to bring it to this lot and throw it in his car. But when I got here, Mr. Rusher was here, so I gave it to him."

At that moment, an ambulance pulled up next to the curb on Oak Lane. The EMTs hopped out and rushed to examine the young actor as Chief Edwards's men hauled the older actor to his feet.

"Oh no," Alice said. "Peggy will be so disappointed."

"Peggy?" Ian looked at her in shock. "Why?"

"Well, with their star in jail, they're probably not going to finish this movie. Peggy won't get to be a star after all."

"She's lucky," Matt Rusher said.

All eyes turned to him.

"I had a great career," he complained. "I made fourteen action movies. I was hotter than Willis, Stallone, and Schwarzenegger combined. Now the studios think I'm too old. All I can find is some drippy cable movie playing the father of a snot-nosed kid!"

Annie glanced at Logan and saw hurt on his face.

"Willis is still making action movies," Rusher said as they hustled him toward the car. "He's no younger than me. And I've still got all my hair! I've still got it! I've still got it!"

Annie could still hear him shouting as they stuffed him in the car and drove away.

20

As Annie dressed the next morning, she thought about how glad she was to be home. Maplehurst Inn was lovely, but Grey Gables felt like she was getting a warm hug from her grandmother all the time. Betsy's loving heart had made its mark on everything. Annie was incredibly glad that very few things had actually been broken in this mystery.

Boots poked her head through Annie's door and began a bossy tirade about the slow breakfast service. At least, Annie assumed that was what the chorus of meows was about.

"No matter where we are, you expect maid service, don't you Bootsie?" Annie asked as she scooped the cat up in her arms.

She was surprised to hear a knock at the front door. She carried the cat with her as she went to answer it. Alice stood at the door, lightly dusted in snow and carrying a basket covered in tea towels. Annie's stomach growled at the sight of it.

Jim stood just behind Alice, grinning his most pirate-like grin.

Annie swung the door open wide. "Come in," she urged. "What brings you guys over?"

"We're celebrating," Alice said.

"Celebrating?" Annie said. "Solving the mystery?"

Alice nodded. "That and I get my car back today. Which

reminds me, can you drive me in for the Hook and Needle Club meeting? Then, take me over to Carson's Body Shop to get my car?"

"Of course," Annie said as she led her friends to the kitchen. "What are you going to do today, Jim?"

"I'm rigging a dark room at Alice's," he said. "The book I'm working on right now is all shot in black and white. I don't trust anyone else with that developing. So, I'm a little behind."

"Oh, Alice," Annie said. "Since Jim is going to be tied up part of his visit with developing photos, do you think you could help me with something?"

"Anything I can."

"I could use a hand bringing some things down from the attic and decorating for Christmas."

Alice raised her eyebrows. "What made you change your mind about decorating?"

"Well, if Mary Beth doesn't mind, I thought I might like to have the Hook and Needle Club Christmas party here."

"I'm sure she wouldn't mind," Alice said, but her look was still quizzical.

"Well, I realized that I might not have LeeAnn and the children here, but I still have family. I have my Stony Point family, and I can decorate for them."

"Then I'm glad to help," Alice said. "But are you sure you're ready to go up to the attic again? We've barely finished one mystery. Who knows what's waiting up there for you?"

Annie put up her hands. "I give up. There's no avoiding these mysteries. You're too adventurous. I'm too stubborn.

And all of us just have too much curiosity for our own good."

"Maybe so," Jim chimed in. "But doesn't it make life fun?"

Laughing at that, they settled down at the table, and Alice unwrapped her basket. The smell of cinnamon and maple wafted off the muffins. "I recognize that aroma," Annie said.

Alice grinned. "Now you get to eat the actual muffins." Alice raised one of the muffins in her hand. "Here's to no more crazy car-bashers!"

"And no more muggings!" Annie added. "Or break-ins."

"And no more snatching of beautiful ladies," Jim added.

The muffins were as good as Annie expected, warm and rich, and stuffed with plump raisins and walnuts. When they'd eaten all they could hold, and nearly all that Alice had brought, Annie finally glanced down at her watch. "Oh no!" she moaned. "We're going to be late for the Hook and Needle Club."

Alice laughed. "Well, that never happens."

They cleaned up the kitchen a little—mostly so Boots wouldn't eat the rest of the muffins while they were gone—and headed for the meeting. The snow of the day before had continued off and on through the night and lay thick on Annie's lawn again. It was a light fluffy snow though, and the high school boy who lived only about a half mile down Ocean Drive had already been by to shovel Annie's steps and drive.

"I'm so glad you told me about Jeremy," Annie said as they got into the snow-dusted car.

"Oh, I know," Alice said. "Every morning when I come outside, and I don't shovel snow, I feel grateful all over again."

The drive to the shop was slow but uneventful. Annie caught Alice leaning over to glance at the speedometer every once in a while. "I'm still nervous of the snow," Annie said.

"Nervous?" Alice said. "Or terrified?"

Annie smiled. "Think of it as helping you really be happy when you get your car back."

When Annie pulled into a parking spot near A Stitch in Time, Alice practically rocketed out of the car. Annie laughed as she followed her friend.

As soon as they got inside the needlework shop, Gwen called out. "You won't believe it! The movie is canceled. They arrested Matt Rusher!"

"Yes," Peggy said. "Apparently he was a thief and a kidnapper! I don't know who he kidnapped yet."

"Me!" Alice said.

The shock on every face made Alice and Annie burst out laughing. Even Stella stopped knitting and stared openmouthed at them. "Too bad Jim couldn't get a photo of that," Annie said.

"You come over here and sit down right now," Gwen said sternly. "We want to hear every detail."

"Did he tie you up?" Peggy asked. "Or worse?"

"Mostly he used duct tape. And I did the 'or worse,'" Alice told them. "I bit him and kicked him pretty hard too." She turned to offer Annie a grin. "We didn't check for those bruises."

Annie just shook her head at her friend. "Apparently he wanted a valise," she said.

"A valise?" Kate yelped. "You mean the one you loaned Vanessa? A kidnapper wanted the bag you gave Vanessa?"

Annie winced. "Technically, we're pretty sure he never wanted that bag, but I'm still sorry. At least she never actually took it. And I still have no idea why he wanted it."

At that Peggy smiled smugly, clearly happy to be back in the know. "I do!" All eyes turned to her and the pretty waitress basked in the attention for a moment before she said. "Well, I'm not naming any names, but two of Chief Edwards's officers were having breakfast at The Cup & Saucer this morning, and they said the chief had pulled the leather cover off some suitcase. They found something right under the leather." Then she paused for dramatic effect, looking from face to face around the group.

"Don't keep us hanging!" Stella exclaimed. "What was it?"

"Letters," Peggy said. "One was from Abraham Lincoln, written on the day he died. It has the date written right on it in his handwriting. And they said there was a letter from John F. Kennedy too, but not on the day he died. Still, apparently it had something scandalous in it. All the letters were from famous dead people."

"Wow, I can imagine those would be worth some money," Alice said.

"And being letters, they would lay so flat we couldn't tell there was anything in the valise," Annie added. "That's why it just seemed empty."

"How did some action-movie actor know about such important pieces of history?" Stella asked.

"I asked the guys that," Peggy said. "Apparently Rusher spilled everything when they waved the letters in his face. He said they belonged to his godmother. Her husband had been some kind of collector, and when she died, he snagged them from her house before her family could get everything cataloged. Then he hid them in a suitcase from her attic."

"How did he end up losing the suitcase?" Mary Beth asked.

"Well, apparently he didn't take it out of the house because he didn't want to risk anyone seeing him leave with the letters. He told the family he wanted the suitcase for sentimental reasons, but they were mad at him, so they never handed it over. He's been trying to track it down for quite a while. He finally found the right relative, and the guy told him he never wanted the suitcase and had dumped it in a thrift store in Boston."

"And that's how it ended up in the props for the movie," Annie said nodding.

"By the time Rusher found the right thrift store," Peggy said. "They'd already sold it to the movie's props department. Apparently Rusher even tried to run the movie's prop master off the road to get the thing."

"Then, when Matt Rusher saw you carrying it in the movie, he thought you had his suitcase," Alice said.

"So he tried to steal it from me when he knocked me down in the snow."

"He knocked you down in the snow?" Mary Beth said. "Why didn't we hear about this?"

"Oh—is that how you got your knees scraped?" Peggy asked.

"Yes. The incident didn't seem all that important at the time," Annie admitted. "Then, of course, Alice's car was all banged up when Rusher tried to force us off the road to get the valise."

"Oh, heavens," Gwen said. "Were you hurt?"

"No," Alice admitted. "But you should have seen what that man did to my Mustang! I hope they put him in prison for a long time!"

"OK, is that when he kidnapped Alice?" Mary Beth asked. She was beginning to look a little confused as she tried to sort out all the events correctly.

"No," Alice said. "He did that when he forced me off the road the next day. I was on the way to the body shop. My poor car!"

Annie explained then how they'd exchanged her valise for Alice, since that's what he demanded. "But of course, there was nothing hidden in my valise. It was really just an old empty suitcase Betsy kept in the attic."

"That must have driven him crazy," Alice said. "No wonder everyone in the movie complained about how cranky he was."

"Serves him right," Stella said with a sniff. "Imagine if the valise had been destroyed in one of those moves over the years. Then those priceless pieces of history would have been lost."

"What did he intend to do with them?" Gwen said.

"The police said he had a buyer," Peggy chimed in, happy to be back in the spotlight. "He was going to sell them and then leave the country. He told Chief Edwards that he had intended to run out on the movie all along."

Annie nodded. "Well, he clearly hated the idea of playing some young actor's father in a sentimental made-for-TV movie."

"He'll probably sell the story of all this to a studio and

get it made into a film," Alice said.

"Oh, wouldn't that be interesting!" Peggy said. "Who do you think would play Matt Rusher, since he'll be in prison?"

Annie and Alice looked at each other, grinned and in unison almost shouted: "Bruce Willis!"

Learn more about Annie's fiction books at

AnniesFiction.com

- Access your e-books
- Discover exciting new series
- Read sample chapters
- Watch video book trailers
- Share your feedback

We've designed the Annie's Fiction website especially for you!

Plus, manage your account online!

- Check your account status
- Make payments online
- Update your address

Visit us at AnniesFiction.com